LOVE IS

MAGICAL

TRUE LOVE NEVER LIE

CHAPTER 1

Wonderfully clear and still cold, the day was beautiful. In this little city of 80,000 people in the Mid West, the winter had been particularly long, rainy, and cold. The students of the little university traveled from building to building every day, and the late March breeze still gave off hints of the winter winds that had ravaged at them. Before graduation and the end of the spring semester, the sunshine gave a preview of the pleasant weather to come.

It was a day that both of our key players would remember for years to come, but for different reasons.

For the spring, Joseph Stevens was prepared. He was a senior in the business administration program and was about to receive his diploma. He was a dedicated student who was determined to acquire his diploma in four years rather than the typical five or six years that it takes for students to complete an undergraduate degree. He was 23 years old, had missed a year of school to earn money for tuition, and was determined to do it.

Additionally, he had a full-time job at a clothing store that catered to young people. Although the university and the corporate office for the network of 300 clothing stores were in the same town, he had begun his career there. He had worked in both retail and distribution, had even assisted with picture shoots for various clothing lines, and knew how to create the distinctive t-shirts that were popular. He was happy that a few of his concepts had turned into popular, seemingly ageless, online t-shirts that sold well.

He had been promised a speedy promotion by his bosses after he had earned the required minimal degree, and he was on track to become the assistant manager of the neighborhood store. He already had plans to get his MBA because the company was both large enough for him to establish a career there and small enough for him to stand out from the crowd. That is, if you were a person who was driven by goals.

Even though the institution had excellent teams, Joseph couldn't recall ever going to a sporting event there because he didn't have much opportunity to socialize with other students outside of class. Maybe the final football game of his junior year was the last event he went to. He had played wide receiver for the first three years of his career, but due to an eye injury that made it difficult for him to focus on the ball while it was in flight, he reluctantly decided to leave the squad and put more of an emphasis on his academics. Additionally, he didn't have time to go to any other extracurricular events.

He was his route to his next class, a required history class, when he made contact with the person who would change his life. He was wearing one of his distinctive t-shirts, a pair of board shorts, and cross trainers. He was also shivering in the breeze.

He was giving his mass to a cute coed who was dressed in sweats and a hooded sweatshirt. Instead of the normal PC or iPad with the essential textbooks downloaded, she was carrying a big suitcase full of books. She was somewhat hunched over from the weight of the entire backpack, and when she collided with a 180-

pound former wide receiver, her overbalance made her easy to knock to the ground.

Both people would recall Joseph's opening remark to the marketing major. "I'm really sorry, oh my God. I didn't pay attention to where I was heading." The student's rucksack had opened, throwing some of her books onto the ground next to her as she sat on her attractively shaped bottom. The fact that some of her loose papers were now drifting in the breeze was more unsettling than her painful behind. In the midst of the white papers flapping in the breeze was her most recent paper due in the following class.

"Not my paper, oh no. Could you please help me get them back? "was Haley's opening remark to Joseph.

He started chasing after the misplaced bits of paper while nodding. He jumped and dove for the paper, displaying his athleticism. Although he made an effort to avoid doing so, every now and then a corner would get slightly wadded as he went on to the next sheet of paper. As soon as the two had all the documents back, they headed inside together so that Haley could organize them.

They organized and reorganized Haley's backpack silently so she could go to class. After finishing, they both realized they were running behind schedule for their subsequent classes, so they went back to the common area where Joseph grabbed a coffee for himself and a latte for Haley.

After removing his brown hair off his eyes, Joseph extended his hand. He had very blue eyes, and Haley wondered if they were real or tinted contacts. She had a query, but she didn't ask for an answer. "My name is Joseph. I'm really sorry to have met you in this situation."

Smiled back at Haley. "Hello, I'm Haley. Although my butt could be sore for a few days, it wasn't a bad way to meet." Haley sat back and gave Joseph a little moment of attention. "We may have taken a few classes together this year, I believe. If you're not compelled to seat somewhere else, you usually sit toward the rear of the room, right?"

Joseph gave a nod. "I try to arrive to class early so that I can study briefly before the lesson begins if I can find a seat close to the entrance. If the lecturer mandates alphabetical seating, I can't study as effectively when seated in the front."

Haley also had a vaguely similar appearance. She fit the description of a pretty next-door neighbor. She didn't have a slender model figure; rather, she had the toned, fit body of a cheerleader. He couldn't quite see how big her breasts were because of her sweats and hoodie, but he had never been a breast man. He wasn't interested in the girl specifically because of her appearance. He had always been drawn to Haley's smile since it was so attractive. He interpreted a broad, sincere smile as a reflection of the person's outlook on life. A girl who smiled frequently and easily usually found life to be great and fascinating. He wouldn't want to spend much time with someone who always had a frown on their face because it usually indicated a negative attitude on life.

He couldn't really tell what color Haley's hair was because she kept her hood up, but he thought it was dark and her brown eyes were expressive. She was also well-known to him, but he had never had the chance to sit next to her in a class they both attended. They had never met in any other college context because he put in so much time outside of class.

They talked and got to know one another a little during the hour. Haley informed him of her major, marketing, and Joseph informed her that she was a part of the second-largest group of business administration students on campus. When he said that his degree would make him qualified as a salesman, they both chuckled. Haley responded, "Even so, that is still preferable to a degree in classical literature. You will only be hired to flip burgers if you do that." On that one, they had concurred.

The hour passed far too quickly. They soon had to split ways. Both exchanged well wishes and the necessary phrases. "See you later." They split up and moved on.

The following several days when they were walking between courses, they would nod at one another. Even when they were accompanied by a group of pupils, they would occasionally pause and speak briefly. Even in their one shared class this past semester, Haley found herself relocating closer to Joseph's seat. They were seated next to each other after spring break.

After spending a week sitting next to each other, Joseph had to ask Haley to switch seats because he was no longer able to concentrate before class started. Although he asked quite nicely, he was aware that it might have damaged her a little. He made an effort to justify his dedication to obtaining his degree by saying that it would be essential to his future with the clothing firm, where he worked when he wasn't in class.

Haley struggled to comprehend. She put in sporadic hours in her father's tire and auto repair shop, helping to schedule repairs but more for the experience of working with the public than for the money. She had always been well-liked and was frequently pursued by men. Compared to the typical horn dogs she was familiar with, her friendship with Joseph was really distinctive. Because her father owned several businesses and was fairly wealthy, some people were drawn to her. Some wanted to screw her because they liked how she looked. But few simply sat and conversed with her. Even Haley's boyfriend at the time, Arthur Jones, or Arthur to his friends, seemed more interested in talking about being the starting quarterback than having a meaningful conversation with her.

Despite the fact that Haley never tried to hide her relationship with Arthur from Joseph, she didn't know why he never asked her out. She never noticed him peering at her tits, and he never appeared to be staring at her ass. She was a little irritated by his lack of interest in her body as a young lady, but her more mature self admired his restraint and maturity.

She did some research, learned about his injury, and learned from Arthur that Joseph had always been a bit of a loner. Except when necessary by the coaches, he had never participated in team activities and had never rushed the fraternity to which the majority of the squad belonged.

Even during his practice sessions, he had kept the current problem in mind. In the locker room or on the field, Joseph had never engaged in any horseplay. To maintain a good GPA, he never enrolled in any easy classes. He wasn't a great player, but he was adequate. They didn't really miss him last year, though.

Naturally, Arthur was immediately envious of any male relationship with his girl when Haley asked him about Joseph. As a result, she rapidly learned to avoid mentioning their platonic chats and her seat in class.

Joseph and Arthur did not share a class because Arthur's major was in communications. When his football career was done, he planned to land a job as a sportscaster. Of course, he had dreams of making the pros, just like the majority of players. He would have a secure financial future and a significantly improved resume even if he could only play for a few years at that level. He might be a color man on a global scale. He constantly worked on his speaking and diction, even when he was playing the game.

Haley and Arthur were intimately involved physically as well. The two would "make love," in Arthur's words, in a hotel room off campus whenever he could. When they first started dating, Haley believed that their sessions together were lovemaking, but she was now coming to the realization that there wasn't much romanticism or foreplay. More of it was just fucking.

CHAPTER 2

When Haley and Arthur first started dating, she wasn't a virgin. No, prom night had taken care of that tiny obstruction to a life of sensual pleasure. Yes, she had erroneously thought that Lukas Benson, a quarterback who she had dated in her senior year of high school, was her soul mate and that she was over heels in love. She had disregarded the advice from her friends that he merely wanted to fuck her and then forget about her. She was a member of the dance team and played clarinet in the band, but she was unable to reach the varsity cheerleading squad, which is why Lukas was drawn to her. They began dating when he chased her. Over time, Lukas had introduced her to necking and given her the necessary hickeys on her neck to the amusement of her girlfriends and to the dismay of her parents. He then moved on to massage her breasts both over her clothes and subsequently with her top unbuttoned and her bra pushed up. When she had to change in the locker room after physical education, her girlfriends once more tittered with delight as he graduated to licking her nipples and moved the hickey spot to her breasts. But she managed to keep these signs of affection a secret from her parents.

He then showed her his "huge" cock, which was only around 5 inches long when fully extended. While they necked at the neighborhood make-out place, he showed her how to stroke his cock. He showed her how to unzip his jeans so that he could aid his cock escape without the zipper hurting or damaging it. He also persuaded her to suck his cock, but she refused since, in her innocence, she thought it was a disgusting thing to do. While he attempted to practically get into her pants, he had to be content to have her stroke him.

There, he didn't have much success. She liked wearing jeans, and he occasionally got to massage her virgin pussy over them, but he couldn't persuade her to unzip them or pull them down. When the weather allowed, she would occasionally wear shorts, but they weren't quite loose enough for him to reach under and touch her exposed, pussy lips. She would only get really red when he asked while licking her nipples as hard as possible. He had no idea if she was clean shaved, naturally hairy, or trimmed. He wasn't even sure if she was becoming overly aroused by their necking.

She also refused to fully stroke his erection. She didn't have enough experience to know what teasing might do to a boy in heat, so she would leave him hanging when she thought he was satisfied. He frequently felt "blue balls" as a result of the abrupt end to their necking so that she could go home on time. Each time, in order to safely continue the journey home, he had to pull over onto a quiet side street and stroke off his load of adolescent sperm. For their dates, he really began to dress in boxers and shorts so that he would have "room to develop," so to speak.

He ultimately persuaded her to complete the stroke the week before prom. To avoid having any sperm stains to explain to anyone, he completely removed his boxers and shorts. Haley never had a brother, therefore she never had the opportunity to discover rags and socks filled with sperm. She was unsure of the precise outcome when a guy would experience this final eruption and cause such a mess. The feeling of holding an erection in her palm as it grew and twitched as he became more and more excited was brand-new and, she had to admit, fascinating. Of course, her health class had taught her what an orgasm was and how an egg became fertilized, but she had never actually done it.

Lukas was on the verge of exploding as she glided up and down while holding his cock. She rejected his repeated attempts to convince her to lick his cock. In order to reduce friction and increase pleasure, he finally succeeded in getting her to lick his cock and her hands with some saliva.

His arousal increased, and he began to hump up into her hand. She controlling his orgasm was something he both loved and dreaded. It was more thrilling than when he could direct the action by using his own hand or caressing an eager pussy, but it was frustrating since he couldn't control the tightness and pace of her hand movements. He was getting more and more thrilled as he got closer. He yelled and fired a massive amount of semen out of the little opening at the end of his cock while his heart was thumping in his ears. He spurted up and then sideways at Haley as she released her hold because she was so startled. Later, she discovered numerous stains from the foul spill on her blouse and shorts.

Lukas let out a second brief snort of fear when Haley stopped stroking his cock because he was so shocked, and then he grabbed his cock and finished his orgasm. His hands soon became covered in semen, and it began to drip onto the seat and the floor.

His sole remark was, "Shit, shit, shit, how am I going to get this all cleaned up?" Haley was staring at the vast amount of white, bleach-smelling fluid with wide eyes. She was silently wondering if this was a typical ejaculation and how anyone could possibly handle the mess. Given that Lukas seemed a little irritated over the mess, she decided against asking.

The two got to work cleaning the vehicle and improving its odor. They had considerable success. Lukas drove Haley home before continuing to his house, rolling down the windows to let the early spring evening air in.

Lukas was pleased with his progress—however slow—in getting inside Haley's underwear. Hopefully the prom romance would be the final straw, leading her to give up her maidenhead. When he took Haley to her door and kissed her passionately, he had a cheery grin on his face as he drove home. If he had known that she had not been at all seduced by the date that evening, he might have been a bit less giddy. Lukas had been more interested in himself than she was.

However, prom night was unique. This was the night that transformed her from a girl to a woman, just like it did for many virgins across the nation. Everything was intended to make it a beautiful evening, including the expensive dress that was only worn once and looked just like a future wedding gown, the corsages, which were most participants' first-ever prom-related accessory, the banquet, and finally the dance.

Except for this one night, most females would never wear something that exposed so much bare shoulder and cleavage. Then came the first-time tuxedo date with an anxious young guy, the potential need to affix the corsage to the dress' bodice, the obligatory family photos, and finally the dinner. Some young women attended their first supper with proper forks and linen napkins at this event. The chicken was chilly and rough, but who cared? Remember, prom was tonight. The dance then started. Although ankles and feet were kicked and trampled on, this was prom, and the majority of the lads had no idea how to dance correctly. Haley was fortunate in that Lukas's mother had made him take ballroom dance classes. Her feet and ankles were not abused. A real disco ball was suspended above the dancers and the school gym was decorated with balloons, streamers, strobe lights, and other decorations. Overall, a romantic fantasy realized.

The customary post-prom parties followed the promenade. One was accompanied and funded by the parents of the juniors. After passing a breathalyzer test, couples were allowed to enter and mingle. The punch was frequently tampered with, but it contained so little alcohol that you had to repeatedly use the restroom to alleviate a hurting bladder before feeling any buzz. But someone was always attempting to generate publicity.

Since this post-prom gathering had the highest attendance, Haley and Lukas went. They could count on seeing all of their pals there.

CHAPTER 3

Haley was welcome to remain as long as she wished during this celebration, which could go on until daybreak.

around 3 a.m. Lukas convinced her to go so they could be by themselves. Haley was still very much of the mindset that nothing bad could possibly happen. Free from the restrictions of high school, she experienced adulthood.

Lukas brought a bottle of inexpensive wine when they arrived at the limo. The limo driver had a few disposable wine glasses that everyone drank from, and soon there was a buzz. When the family got together, Lukas's parents always let the youngsters have a beer, but Haley wasn't used to any alcohol and quickly became tipsy. The back of the limousine was a fantastic place for a seduction. The back of the limousine was illuminated with colourful lights that gave it an unreal radiance. The comfy, spacious seats were ideal for some horizontal Mombo time. Additionally, a privacy cover shielded the driver's view of the back. Lukas erected it and gave the motorist the go-ahead to simply cruise.

Haley seemed cheerful and a touch inebriated. She was also relaxed and open to Lukas's attention. He kissed her repeatedly before kissing her ear and murmuring how much he wanted her to experience the entirety of this magnificent night. Haley sighed as she nodded. Her dress' zipper was opened by Lukas, revealing her bare breasts underneath. Haley was emitting delicious tiny sighs

15

and soft moans as he licked and nibbled at her flawless rose-red nipples till they stood hard and wet from his saliva.

He quickly began pulling up her skirt and groping about in her wet panty crotch. Despite the transparent fabric, he rubbed her nub. He was startled to see that she had lace panties on tonight rather than cotton ones. He may have underestimated how ready she was to lose her maidenhead. The idea made his cock tighten.

He persisted in softly stroking her pussy and sucking her nipples till she groaned in annoyance. Though she hadn't often had the urge to masturbate, she understood that there was a limit to how long she could continue to play the fool. This time, Lukas's delicate strokes had to pick up their pace or stop completely. Please go harder, her drunken brain begged.

She wasn't even conscious that she had spoken it aloud. Indulging his forefinger inside her underwear, Lukas grinned at her before feeling her deliciously warm and moist pussy for the first time. Of course, he was used to this by now. This was merely odd for him because he had been with numerous girls and a few adult women. When she felt someone else touching her bare skin for the first time, she gasped. He had no obstacle to overcome because her pubic hair was so scanty that she had never thought to shave it. He quickly began to rub her erect little "guy in the boat" with his index finger. Haley quickly started to orgasm and had to grasp his hand to stop him from making her hurt. "Please pause for a moment. I need to take a breath after that; it was too intense."

Lukas gave in and simply held his finger on the tip of her clit and slowly moved it around while he sucked on her neck and gave her shivers of pleasure from that different erogenous zone since he knew he was getting near to the prize. He offered her a brand-new gizmo to show off to her pals. Before the night was done, he hoped to have the opportunity to get one closer to her vagina. Her locker room friends would be shocked by it. The idea almost made him chuckle.

She was soon prepared again, and after soaking his finger in her pussy fluids initially, he started to finger more vigorously. In this type of manual sex, lubrication was crucial. With the stimulation, she began to sweat and move her hips. Lukas kept making inconsequential remarks in her ear. Even just the warm breath was stimulating. The pleasure was further enhanced by his comments, which described how he wanted her to feel so amazing, how he wanted to be her main man, how wet her pussy was, and how heavenly he felt her breasts were.

This time, as she approached the pinnacle and prepared to leap off the pleasure cliff, he sometimes worked more slowly to increase her intensity and her need. Lukas thought the time was right when she began to moan a little about how she wanted an orgasm or she would have to call it a night. As she reclined on the plush leather seat, her whole skirt was up and her bodice was down. Due to his skilled manipulation and her climax, her virginal pussy was wet and open. By the time she understood what Lukas was doing, he was rubbing her lips and nubbin as his cock head was getting

17

moist. He quickly rushed forward and pierced her tight, virgin pussy on the first strike as she regained control and began to stop him.

She screamed in anguish at the sudden entrance and the loss of her hymen, but the pain soon subsided. Lukas made sure to wiggle his pelvis against hers and pound his pubic bone against it before pulling back and impaling her once more. The force of his hammering thrusts and the sensation of him penetrating her made her tremble. He froze with his cock buried as deeply as he could before shuddering and groaning as he poured his semen into her open gash just as it was starting to feel wonderful.

After that, he withdrew, leaving a rope of semen connecting his cock to her vagina. Haley was trying to figure out what she was meant to do when he fell back. She was still ecstatic in a sexual way, but also annoyed. Then, I imagined how wanton she must have appeared with her tits exposed, her pussy wide open, and semen beginning to leak out as her dress was up over her head. She crossed her legs and lowered her dress' skirt. She was appalled by what had happened. Even with a boy she thought she was in love with, she wasn't ready to commit fully.

Lukas flashed her a contented smirk as he turned to face his most recent victim. "Hey, Baby, wasn't it the best thing you've ever experienced? You're a hot fuck, dude. The wait has been worthwhile, and we can now fuck whenever we want."

Haley was hearing things that she couldn't believe. Lukas had changed from the sexy kid who only wanted to fuck to the one who had been speaking lovely loving things into her ears while she was being turned on by him. Her attitude quickly shifted.

She sat up and made an effort to hide her exposed breasts. She had long since forgotten anything about sex. "Lukas, take me home now. I have to get there as quickly as I can."

Lukas made an attempt to soothe her, but the recently descended former virgin didn't take kindly to his remarks about how they could fuck constantly.

Haley knocked on the wall after putting some order in the top of her dress. She provided the driver her address and instructed him to take her home when it came down. Lukas shook his shoulders in response to the driver's look. Tonight, he would make her laugh. In the end, he got to implant his sperm deep inside her pussy as the freshly worked muscles flitted around his shaft. For the rest of her life, she would keep this in mind. He would soon persuade her to meet with him again.

Because her parents believed she was heading to the sponsored all-night post-prom party and wouldn't return until dawn, Haley was able to sneak into their home without being seen. The gown was discolored, and some of the seams were torn, so she dumped it into the trash bin and hoped her mother wouldn't check too closely. She then took a lengthy shower to clean herself up before giving herself an unplanned douche with the handheld sprayer to get rid of any lingering semen. Her underwear was promptly hand cleaned in the shower as well and placed right away in a hamper wrapped in a towel to partially dry. Haley thought her mother

CHAPTER 4

Wouldn't see the inappropriate personal clothing because she did her own laundry.

The tiredness Haley had after the Saturday night festivities allowed her to fall asleep. She was sexually satisfied, therefore she didn't sleep. The last thing she wanted at the conclusion of this weekend was an orgasm. She had to get up and study before classes on Monday when she woke up in the late afternoon.

Of course Mitchell's mother was interested in every detail of the prom. She lovingly recalled the prom she had attended many years prior when she had triumphed as prom queen and her then-boyfriend Austin had been crowned prom king next to her. She recalled the post-prom gatherings as well as the shared room they had at a nearby motel where the couple practiced making love. Months before, they had each given the other their virginities, but this night of nights marked their first opportunity to share a bed. They didn't get married until after college, although Austin had proposed to her that evening.

Haley was able to tell her mother about the dresses, the amazing banquet, the dancing, and of course some of the antics that took place even if she wasn't aware of everything her parents did on their prom night. Some of the youngsters couldn't enter since they were so inebriated when they arrived. The next few weeks would not be fun for the boys who were guilty but their dates weren't, as many couples broke up because the girls were allowed in and went on stag weekends while their immature boyfriends sat outside in the parking lot and grew more inebriated contemplating how they had been hoping to strike it lucky until they failed the sobriety test. Even the girls who were anticipating a romantic evening with the prospect of sharing intimate moments with their soul mates were now pessimistic. Because their boyfriends had to drink that night of all nights, their plans were shattered. Why couldn't they hold off on getting shitfaced until graduation? On graduation night, nobody looked forward to getting fucked.

They laughed a lot about how immature some boys were and how some girls only cared about getting attention. Haley didn't elaborate much about Lukas and their specific actions. She also failed to inform her mother when she arrived home. She let everyone believe she had spent the entire evening at the post-promparty.

She slept better on Sunday night and was more prepared than normal to start school on Monday. She typically had Lukas take her up, but this time she chose to walk to a friend's house and then call a ride. It was advantageous. When she arrived at school, she saw that Lukas had left. He was chit-chatting a freshman in an effort to graduate with at least one more notch on his bedpost.

Except for the tales that Lukas started about how she was a chilly bitch and a lousy fuck, Haley wasn't too offended. For the following week, she maintained her composure and kept her pals close until a fresh piece of juicy rumor caught everyone's eye.

Lukas sought to replicate their prom date with Haley just before graduation. After deflowering the freshman, he struck up a conversation with her and found her wanting. He was determined to assist Haley in gaining the requisite experience because he was aware that she would ultimately make a better sex partner if she had more. He quickly lost hope in a repetition when Haley publically reprimanded him before severely kneeing him in the nuts, leaving him with sore nuts. The hallway was filled with laughter at his expense.

Haley's summer after high school graduation was uneventful. She periodically ran components to the other shops in her father's chain while working as a counter person at her father's main tire and car repair building. She was a cheerful person who gave her job her all, but she was also mature enough to recognize that it was redundant at best and that the only reason she had a job was because she was the boss's daughter. Haley wasn't overindulged at all. She was punctual for work and offered assistance with any tasks that needed doing, but she was aware of her privilege. She always had a car to drive, obviously with her name on the title, but with Daddy paying the bill. She always had cash on hand to spend and a credit card that she could use without incurring debt.

On occasion, she could leave work early to attend a party with her girlfriends. She dated seldom and never truly connected with any other boy. She now distrusted most boys because of Lukas. She was open to dating an older man, but he would need to be more responsible. She wasn't in a rush to date because she thought she would meet a more mature person at the nearby institution where she was attending.

She was about to embark on a brand-new scholastic experience when courses began in the fall. Since the university was in her hometown, she had assumed she was familiar with it, but she soon discovered that it was more like a distant nation. There was this sudden influx of a really diverse group of individuals from all over the world, including students, faculty, and even staff. She swiveled her head from side to side as she waited in line to register for classes and pick up school supplies on her first day to try to take in all of the languages, dialects, slang phrases, fashion trends, skin colors, and personality types of the individuals she would be going to school with.

Some of her high school classmates were there, but because they were enrolled in different subjects and had less time for socializing, she quickly realized that they were busy forging new relationships.

It's time to hang out as they did in high school. She also made the decision to attempt continuing her clarinet lessons, although finding the time to do so was quite challenging. Only the music majors appeared to have the time to perform and practice. She made the hasty decision to rule out the extracurricular activity because color guard practices were place during periods when she had to be in class.

She decided to major in marketing since she thought her father may benefit from it for the benefit of the household business. Although just as a family firm, the tire and vehicle repair shops were incorporated. Haley, an only child, believed that in order to contribute to the expansion of the company, she would need to study everything she could. When the time was right, her father, Brian Storm, would teach her how to operate the company his way, but she was aware that he wasn't very good at marketing it to get the most bang for his buck in terms of advertising.

She had to study, but even if the classes were engaging, she wasn't required to do so constantly. She didn't have to worry about paying for tuition, books, or living expenses, but she could still work at the stores to earn some spending money. She even decided against daily commutes from her home to live in the residence halls. She did finally make the decision to join a sorority during Rush Week. She would then volunteer her excess time there. She survived the hazing, which wasn't quite as difficult as it had been when her mother had pledged to the same sorority many years earlier.

When Mitchell and Haley compared notes on the initiation procedure, Haley was relieved that she had not been required to perform as many servile duties as Mitchell had when she had rushed a sorority in college. Since Mitchell was ashamed of how she had to humiliate herself to join the sorority, she concealed the worst memories from her daughter. Since the majority of such practices were now prohibited, sorority members understood better than to take advantage of pledges to such an extent.

In college, Haley occasionally went out on dates. Each female sought to find a fraternity member or different classmate to take to the specified event because each partner sorority and fraternity offered several events that required dates. The Student Affairs

Council hosted numerous dances and concerts, which encouraged the lads to ask young women to go with them. They were all platonic. There were also the study sessions that devolved into pizza fests, where a group would place a large order for pizza as a break, and some individuals would pair off while dining and just hang out with each other. Overall, Haley had a busy first year and wasn't prepared for any relationships.

She met Arthur at the start of her second year. He was drawn to her because she wasn't the kind to swoon upon meeting the star quarterback. At a fraternity party, he noticed her from across the room, and she didn't appear to be bothered by the throng of ladies vying for his attention. Arthur always found it amusing how out of control certain women would act when attempting to attract a man's attention. If he was stag, there was always the possibility of a brawl at a party between two girls who had chosen he was the one for them. He soon discovered that when attempting to break up conflicts, he should avoid the fingernails and pointed teeth.

Arthur was another affluent young man. Since junior high, his physical prowess had made life simpler for him. His friends, students, and even teachers seemed to go above and beyond to help him with homework, studying, and even test taking once he was named to the starting lineup of any team. With Communications as his major, life wasn't all that difficult, even though the work was a little harder now that he was in college and more professors were resistant to his popularity. Even away games didn't interfere with his academics because the college was able to make classes available to all student athletes over the internet.

It was unexpected to transition from high school to collegiate sports. He found college athletics, especially at this tiny campus, to be particularly focused on a single sport per athlete, in contrast to high school athletics when he played in many sports during the school year. While he continued to attend team meetings and receive year-round coaching in football, he might have continued to run with the track team or swing a bat in an intramural baseball game to keep in shape. This wasn't a hobby; it was more like a true career. His sophomore season saw him selected as the starting quarterback after toiling on the sidelines his initial year. He was being instructed and given tips on how to read the defense, stand, pass, look for open receivers, and run if necessary. Every week, there were brand-new plays. Game films were examined in order to learn as much as possible about the opposition's players. He had been a member of the scout squad throughout his freshman year, thus he had to play against the varsity team like the opponents. That served as a painful eye opener.

He was still a huge figure on campus, though. He was praised and recognized everywhere he went. He expected to be recognized, and if someone—especially a coed—didn't seem impressed, something wasn't right and needed to be fixed. One of those wrongs was Haley.

He disbanded the gang and went over to Haley. Instead of making some obscure comment because he didn't even know her name, he just asked her for her name. He greeted her and asked about her major and other interesting details to start the discussion. To the dismay of the other coeds who wanted a piece of the quarterback, the two were soon conversing.

This initial meeting led to dates, and Arthur was knowledgeable enough to let her decide how rapidly things developed. Furthermore, he had a lot of coeds at his disposal if he needed to relieve himself sexually. He didn't endure much time without assistance.

Since neither of them was of legal drinking age, their relationship developed from simple movie dates to going to an underage bar. Additionally, his NCAA rating had to be taken into account at all times. He worked a part-time job that gave him some extra cash. He was given a full scholarship, so he wasn't concerned about accommodation, tuition, or books. Even his dues to the fraternity were covered by a different scholarship. He only required some money for clothes and dating.

By chance, he worked a part-time job at the same shop that Joseph did. Only healthy, average-sized persons were hired because the store made it a point to have workers that could best display its clothes lines. Arthur just wanted to work in sales since it would expose him to the public. Unlike Joseph, he didn't feel the need to research the entire business.

Arthur was a solid quarterback height at 6 feet 1 inch. In addition, he was about 200 pounds and had the strength to resist 300-pound linemen's tackles. He became the face of college sports thanks to his flamboyant blonde hair and intensely blue eyes. The NCAA had frequently exploited his photograph and likeness in their promotional efforts. Additionally, he had been highlighted as a rising star in a number of sports journals. Everyone's perception of him was evolving.

The way Arthur came across didn't concern Haley. He didn't appear to be overly interested in the publicity, which intrigued her. He would casually discuss endorsements and different interviews as though they didn't matter that much to him. Of course, he couldn't yet benefit from any endorsements, but he was already familiar with the principles of public relations. He was being kept under check and within NCAA regulations by an agent, who was obviously not yet being paid. Even though it was a few years away, he planned to sign with him as soon as he graduated.

The bond between Haley and Arthur was strong. When they would eat out, Haley insisted on covering half the bill. It didn't go against NCAA regulations, barely affected her parental money, and allowed them to go out more frequently. On balmy nights, they could stroll around the campus, watch a movie in the dorm lounge, play a game of some sort on TV, play video games (Haley was superb at those so Arthur was constantly challenged), or simply find a quiet spot and neck for a bit.

Arthur was old enough to know better than to stamp his territory on Haley the way a high school punk might. His hickeys would be undetectable while wearing clothing. Placement was a little challenging due to some of his dates' attire selections. When he could, he preferred to suck a beautiful round one directly on the cheek of his date's ass or close to her pussy. Although Haley was unique, the majority of the girls enjoyed that. She had gone through the entire experience with Lukas, so she wasn't looking forward to doing it again. She enjoyed Arthur's nibbling motions on her neck. When someone kissed her neck and ears, she genuinely shook. Even more thrilling was nibbling. After a while, sucking a hickey became just uncomfortable.

Arthur claimed that their romance developed into a physical one, albeit gradually. Haley did not want a situation like Lukas where she was merely a notch on a stud's bedpost. As their dates went on, Arthur and she evolved from a basic goodnight kiss to cuddling on a couch while watching a movie to gradually undressing and examining each other's bodies.

With any other girls he had dated, Arthur had never discovered that he enjoyed having his nipples massaged. As their chemistry deepened, he and Haley would alternate between kissing and nipple-sucking. His cock would react, making his clothes uncomfortable and tight. With her erection, her underwear would get wet, but it wasn't as uncomfortable.

Arthur finally succeeded in getting Haley nude after multiple dates and make-out sessions. They were in a neighborhood motel, and the lights were dim. Arthur was waiting on the bed in just his boxers when Haley emerged from the toilet wearing a sheer nightgown. She had intended to allow him complete access to her body, but he already knew about her sensitive beasts and nipples and had felt her hot young pussy through her pants.

She walked over to the bed's edge and pouted briefly. "You said you'd be waiting for me when I came out in the nude. What's up, Buster, with the boxers?

He made a small chuckle. "I am aware that you are more lovely than I am. I look better with a little clothing on, and even after we decided to share a room for the night, I got the impression that you weren't quite ready to go all in with me. I believed that showing my cock too soon might turn you off. I want this to be delightful in every way and not at all uncomfortable. My boxers will remain on unless you ask me to take them off.

Haley bent down and gave him a kiss after thanking him for considering her comfort level. Then, instead of their customary vertical level, he made room for her on the bed and they started making out horizontally. Their previous relationship allowed both to giggle a little and work to accommodate each other when they made awkward attempts to neck and fondle each other. Arthur was eager to see Haley in her undies but not in a rush. There was no game or class tomorrow. There was time. Because of his prior interactions with girls and women, he was able to restrain some of his urge to perform the deed immediately and place his cock inside of a hot, moist pussy.

CHAPTER 5

Haley was battling the last of her first fucking's demons. She was making an effort to unwind and relish this fresh session of the sexual congress. She massaged Arthur's body, getting into every crevice that was accessible to her. She licked his armpit, another erogenous area he was unaware of, and even laved his chest with her tongue. His cock was responding with her explorations as well, making him shiver with each new feeling. He could see that it was becoming more turgid even if it wasn't fully erect yet.

Haley touched his back and felt his thickly muscled buttocks. His glutes were so toned and tight. Although she didn't say it out loud, she wondered if any girls had ever kissed him there. That would be a topic for an other time. With Arthur, she was certain that this wouldn't be a one-time thing.

At the same time, Arthur was also busy investigating her body. He supported himself on one elbow so that he could examine her generous curves with with one hand. He gently touched her nipples one at a time after massaging her breasts one at a time. He would then proceed to a different place before any titilation could get too powerful and hence frustrating. He also stroked her back. It was really toned and silky. Before continuing, he even made his way down to her small, tight butt and lightly stroked each cheek. He repeatedly kissed his girlfriend as he was doing this. The purpose of these kisses was to seduce them and improve their experience. large amount of tongue movement and an open mouth.

Haley soon started to feel quite heated. She stood up and took off her clothing. Arthur put the closest nipple in his mouth right away, making sure it was firm and upright. He also made a tiny sucking motion at her aureole to see if the glands there would wrinkle up and make her nipple protrude even more. He made it. Haley complained about how happy he was making her feel.

She then assaulted his boxers after being nude. Since they had been dating for a few weeks, she had yet to see Arthur's manhood. She frequently felt his cock through his jeans but never had the nerve to unzip him and look around. Lukas had never given her a chance to get used to the concept of fondling a penis; instead, he had always been aggressive in wanting her to play with his cock.

When she attempted to take off his boxers, Arthur grinned. She was annoyed that she couldn't persuade them to calm down long enough to show his cock because he wasn't currently offering any assistance. She was able to reach his boxers and feel his semi-hard cock, but she was unable to see it. He finally gave up and elevated his pelvis off the bed so the offending clothing could be taken off when she appeared frustrated. Haley breathed a sigh of relief as he was seen for what he was. She assisted in taking off the boxers fully before returning to check his cock.

She then carefully examined it after doing so. She stroked it up and down while holding it to give it more room to grow. He had a well-defined head. The shaft was at least a few inches longer and slightly thicker than Lukas's. When she moved her palm up and down, the tiny aperture at the top gaped. The aperture would develop a little cumulus. She hesitated because she had never done something like before before bending over and sampling the drip. It had a weak flavor but was slightly sticky in texture.

They had spoken about when Haley might be able to engage in oral sex. In her lecture, she had been honest about how Lukas had pushed her to suck his cock, but she had refused and won the struggle. Arthur had reassured her that while he would like to have a love relationship with someone, he did not base any of his relationships on whether or not a female liked him. He was truly eager to do an oral performance for her and was well prepared to do so. No matter how he accomplished the task, he liked it when a girl or woman lost all control.

Additionally, he shared with her his perspective on oral sex, which was that typically, the performer was not the one who was being served. Only in the most extreme pornographic films might you witness a man simply fucking his mouth. If he had any regard for the female, he would have given her full control over his enjoyment. She could make him laugh or sate his lust. She may use her teeth to softly or painfully scratch his cock. She had the ability to mildly or even severely bite his cock. The only one with power was the one offering the pleasure.

He said that she would be in control of any oral sex, and Haley considered putting him in her mouth to make him feel good. She was a little hesitant to let him place his mouth down where she also urinated because she had never done oral sex. She was a little intimidated despite knowing from chatting to her pals that it should be enjoyable.

They kept having fun and exploring. If he could, Arthur would like to hickey her breast. Haley shrugged in opposition. Bruises didn't appeal to her. She did give him the go-ahead to continue titillating her with tiny kisses and nibbles. She sat on her haunches, running her mouth and both hands over his muscular body as she continued to examine him. Before periodically returning to his cock, she tasted his skin all over his front. He would falter slightly from the lack of attention, but with a little effort on her side, he would recover to full hardness.

Arthur could also explore the place he had been eager to see and experience while on her haunches. He became the second boyfriend to prod her pussy by slipping a hand between her legs. He noticed that her outer lips were swollen and bloody. Her clitoris was only the size of a pea and was upright. She lacked a noticeable, big clit. He also immediately massaged her vagina. She was wet when he found her, and his finger entered with ease. With the entrance into her moist pit, Haley sighed once more.

The sensation was not the same as when she used her own fingers to pierce her pussy, despite the fact that she had masturbated a few times over the years. She had no control over the ability to command this odd finger. Another finger soon joined it, and the sensations improved even more. She would jump and groan a little when Arthur periodically withdrew enough to rub her small clit directly. She could tell how he felt about her reaction from his smile. She appreciated him by giving him a passionate, long kiss. She soon found it difficult to focus on his cock as her enjoyment grew. As her climax became closer, she was no longer able to rub his chest because one hand was now supporting her equilibrium. Her eyelashes grew heavy and her breathing became erratic as she carefully stroked his manhood with her other hand. He was aware of her proximity for a variety of factors, including her lack of attention. His fingers were being grabbed by her pussy muscles. She was beginning to jump whenever he ran his finger over her clit, which was growing more sensitive. Her groans were evolving into tiny whines of joy. As her head kept drooping, her hair became more difficult to manage. Even though every muscle in her body was pleading with her to collapse on her back and let him to mount her, her one hard arm was rigid in its need to keep her standing.

Her breathing became more labored, and a blush developed on her neck and chest. She suddenly froze and pressed her hand on his. As it tightened its grip on them, he assumed she was attempting to squirm more into her pussy. She groaned and shook with her first orgasmic outburst of the evening. Lukas was unable to easily accomplish what Arthur did.

She sank down on his chest as she descended from her orgasmic high since her arm could no longer support her weight. She took a little break before turning to meet her new love. "Wow, it was amazing. Never have I experienced anything like it. It went above and beyond anything I had ever been able to achieve for myself.

She gave him a tender kiss after saying that before focusing on his needs. In order to readily reach his cock, she persuaded him to roll to his back once more. As she approached, she lost complete focus, which caused him to lose some of his tumescence. However, as soon as she returned her focus to him, he responded fast once more. As she rubbed him all over, she drew nearer and nearer. She licked her palm before beginning to touch him once more after Arthur told her that a little lubricant would be helpful. This worked for a short while, but as the saliva dried, she had to repeat the lick. She quickly returned to the top of his cock. From his vantage point, Arthur couldn't see her face, but he deduced that she was interested in sucking his cock but still a little reluctant. He was cautious not to approach her or exert any pressure on her. She had to make that choice on her own.

Even if she didn't use her mouth on him, just watching her play with his genitalia was energizing. He was not in control and could only react to what she was doing, just as she was not in control while he toyed with her pussy. That wasn't a problem just now, but when his need to cum increased, failing to manage the sensation would cause an overflow of stimulation.

Then he noticed that his cumin was being tentatively re-tasted by her tongue. She gave it a little swirl around his cockhead before taking it softly in her lips. After giving it a taste, she must not have been put off because she immediately closed her lips around it and began sucking. She took a little more of his cock into her mouth after getting acclimated to the flavor. Since she didn't have much of his cock in her mouth, she began to move up and down a little and let more of her saliva soak the head and top shaft. She feared that she may choke on him.

As she fell in love with Arthur's cock for the first time, he rubbed her back. He was honored that she had put enough faith in him to overcome this hurdle. She had told him on previous dates that sucking cock was not an option, but now, as they were about to have sex, she was sucking him.

She slid a little so he could access her rounded nether cheeks as he stroked down her back, pausing sometimes to cup and massage her nearest breast. She continued to take more and more of his cock into her mouth as he massaged them both and again got between her legs.

Before regaining her pussy once more, he gave her rectum a gentle stroking motion. His three fingers, by this point thoroughly oiled, had little trouble getting inside because she was still fully lubricated. She was doing the same for him as he began to increase her ecstasy level.

Approximately half of his cock was now in her mouth. Her fingers was kept lubricated beneath her mouth by the saliva that was running down his shaft. She was sucking and licking whatever she could with her tongue. On rare occasions, she would remove his cock from her lips and lick the entire shaft all the way down to his nuts. He had hair on them, and she tried licking them a few times, but she didn't like it.

He started to swell in her mouth, tiring her mouth and jaw. He was struggling to restrain himself from needing to pump into her mouth cavity since the sensations were becoming too strong. His legs started to shake, and he started his own sort of a whine, intermingled with groans of pleasure. Haley ignored his attempts to warn her of the necessity for him to cum. She wasn't in danger of losing control and potentially hurting his cock even though he had three fingers jammed into her pussy and his thumb was once again rubbing her clit. She convinced herself that she could swallow his sperm if she could just suck his cock. She lived by the adage "in for a penny, in for a pound." Although she wasn't sure whether she could stand the taste of his sperm, she was determined to find out.

He was losing control, so she couldn't smile while his cock was in her mouth. So she grinned to herself. He was losing the capacity to play with her pussy and his breathing was becoming erratic. His breathing was becoming more rapid and his moans were becoming louder. She felt him growing bigger as his cock grew in her mouth, and he was twitching his legs in an attempt not to impale her neck on his.

A loud spurt of blood struck the back of her throat as he abruptly let out a small scream. She nursed on his cock head and continued to pump up and down on his shaft. She had to swallow the initial spurt right away to prevent choking. She continued to have energy and volume bursts, but she was unable to swallow quickly enough due to a full mouth.

Arthur was stiff for the first three or four spurts, but as Haley finished working him, he began to loosen up. In order to avoid repeating the error she made with Lukas when she stopped stroking his cock as he was approaching, she made careful to continue sucking and stroking. She cleaned his cock head after what appeared to be the final drop appeared to be in her mouth before raising her head.

Because she had his semen on her face and a trickle on her hand from her inability to keep it in her mouth owing to the amount of his spending, she half expected her lover to look at her with contempt as she turned to face him. He moved the hair away from her face, and she was happy to see that his face showed pleasure and affection.

"Wow, that was great, baby. It was your first BJ ever, and you chose to eat the entirety of my cum. I admire the woman you are. She washed her face and hastily cleaned her hands. After saying "thank you," Arthur gave her a fervent kiss. It was now his time. She sighed and shivered when he gently nipped her neck one more. He gave each breast equal time with his hands, lips, tongue, and teeth as he then tenderly made love to her breasts. Without any external stimulation, her nipples were firm and erect once more. Then he made her lay flat on the bed and started licking her stomach, moving down her leg until he sucked her great toe, before switching to the other leg and working his way back up to her calling pussy. The lips were slightly apart and it was damp. Though he couldn't see her "guy in the boat," he was perfectly aware of its exact location under the car's hood. He gently licked her, gauging how rough to be with her by the sigh of contentment and pleasure she sent out.

He forced apart her outer lips and licked the little collection of liquid that had formed at its base. She was just as mouthwatering as he had anticipated. He licked each lip upward and then downward twice. He would repeatedly pause and tickle her clit, causing her pelvis to sway in anticipation of additional stimulation. He then felt sorry for her and got up when she started panting and requesting her orgasm. Once again set for action, his erection. He directed it to her almost virgin opening and speared her carefully. He moved in by an inch before moving back to where he was barely touching her. then move in another inch before exiting. He continued doing this until he was completely enclosed in her cozy container. She grunted in satisfaction at the sensation his cock was giving her. Comparing this to Lukas was like night and day. Arthur carefully withdrew and then slipped home again, determined that this would be enjoyable for them both. On the in-stroke, he made sure his pelvic bone would come into contact with her erected clit. On rare occasions, he would even grind against her mons while cradling her with his cock. He was the perfect length.

The Goldilocks comparison made her chuckle. Arthur was the perfect size, whereas Lukas was too little. She wasn't sure if it could be "just right" because she had never played with a truly big cock, but she was content in the moment. She was soon grasping his hips with her legs and pulled him tight as she experienced her second orgasm of the evening as Arthur worked her and practically played her like a harp, striking each note just on pitch with the perfect pluck.

She sobbed and writhed against his body, shifting her pelvis up and down and back and forth as she devoured every last millimeter of his cock. Her chest was a deep crimson color from her eagerness, and her arms were tightly gripping his shoulders. She pressed her chest up against his so she could enthusiastically massage his chest hair with her nipples. With her third orgasm, that tiny bit of stimulation transported her back into Never, Never Land, where she whimpered and sobbed a little.

Soon she was exhausted. He repeatedly drove in and out as she relaxed and turned into a puddle of flesh with her legs spread wide and her pussy lips fluttering around his cock. She said, "Thank you," as she slowly opened her eyes. Her satisfaction had filled her lids, but she was still eager to take part in the second fucking of her life.

With each strong cock thrust, she grunted. She meowed a little as he moved away. She would have purred if she had the ability. She giggled again, wondering whether this was the reason her vagina was referred to as a pussy. It desired to purr in contentment.

As long as he could, Arthur continued. He would try to position her differently the next time, but this time he wanted to watch her

41

face as he dug her narrow, wet furrow. His muscles in his arms and legs shook as his cock grew by a tiny bit further, signaling his impending peak. He then spit his semen into her plump and receptive pussy. She almost convinced herself that she could actually feel his warm sperm entering her womb. She was fortunately protected by her oral medications and was past ovulation this month nonetheless.

His cock was held in place by her inner muscles until it gradually lost all stiffness and fell out of her pussy. She just rolled to her side and giggled once again as a stream of spermy semen followed it. She needed to get up and do some cleaning, but her orgasms and his loving affection had left her exhausted. She quickly approached sleep and decided to spend the night in the dreadful wet spot.

Arthur gave her a tender kiss and massaged her breasts and arms. They quickly disappeared into dreamland once he covered them both.

They continued to date and have little sex encounters here and there all year. During the summer, Arthur visited his hometown, and they kept up a regular correspondence. What a blessing for their relationship Skype and Facetime were. They could see one other whenever they wanted, and occasionally they made sexual advances toward one another. When classes resumed, they were prepared to rekindle their romance and did so. Before Haley and Joseph ran into each other, they dated practically exclusively, or at least Haley thought they were exclusive.

CHAPTER 6

Haley was unaware that Arthur treated her like a queen as much as he could given his financial limits while they were dating. They had sex but didn't act too naughtily toward one another. When Haley said "No," Arthur respected her. However, he would occasionally go to the bar and pick up one or more other coeds for wild, unrestrained sex in which the girl or girls never said "No" to any act.

Prior to meeting Joseph, Haley was thinking about accepting Arthur's marriage proposal. Like Haley had been to Arthur, Joseph was a mystery to Haley. She questioned why Joseph had never attempted to touch her physically despite the fact that they could talk for hours on end about anything. For a modern, emancipated woman, this should have been the ideal relationship, but Haley was perplexed.

She didn't believe Joseph was homosexual; in fact, she had the exact opposite opinion. His peaceful attitude and rugged good looks drew her in. She was aware that he didn't have to be effeminate to be gay, but she went with her gut instinct that he was a simmering volcano who was just waiting for the right lady to set him off.

She had come to the conclusion that Joseph had been hurt by at least one prior girlfriend while they were talking about personal matters unrelated to their lessons. He made hints that he had been in committed relationships, but that due to the lack of trust, all sentiments of love had also been gone.

His disinterest in her physical characteristics struck Haley as a challenge. She respected him when he asked her to move to a different seat at the start of each session so he could study undisturbed, but she began to dress a little more formally. As the weather warmed, she would don tighter pants and tank tops. When they were together, she occasionally stretched and yawned so that her breasts would be proudly exposed beneath their thin covering. She would make a show of taking off her jacket and draping it over the back of her chair once she was alone with him on a cool day.

When she realized he was looking at her breasts, she would get a little red. She was aware that he appreciated them, but he never complimented her appearance. She kept looking for compliments, but he never got the message. She was dissatisfied.

But once, when she spoke about something unimportant, she carelessly stroked her breast while wearing a skimpy shirt. Joseph assured her that he would never make an effort to initiate a serious relationship with a female who was already in one. She knew then to slightly lower her voice. They reverted to being just casual friends.

That changed a few weeks before to the end of the school year and graduation. When her anxieties were allayed, Haley had been awaiting and dreading Arthur's marriage proposal. One evening, Arthur arrived to her sorority house to inform her that he would be a free agent since he had not been selected in the NFL draft. He would need to relocate to one of the major cities with a franchise before taking seriously his chances of obtaining a slot machine. He confessed his love to her but expressed his concern that his way of life would not be suitable for her. Money would be even tighter than it was before, and it was unclear when and if things would improve.

Haley was simultaneously relieved and devastated since she realized she didn't love Arthur enough to propose marriage. A voice in the back of her head was urging her to throw Joseph to the ground and see what may happen.

They agreed to stay in touch even after graduation, but they both understood that wasn't going to happen—at least not right now.

After things with Arthur were settled, Haley moved on to pursue her next suitor. Joseph Stevens was the target of her attention.

She made sure to indicate that Arthur was relocating after graduation and why when they next got together for coffee and conversation about their common class. She told Joseph that she was staying put when he asked what her plans were. She stated that Arthur will soon find a replacement for her and that her dad wanted her here to assist with the business.

She leaned in close to Joseph and admitted that she wasn't really devastated over Arthur. "I believe Arthur was what I needed to help me move past Lukas's treatment of me and gain some maturity along the way. Although he is a little one-dimensional, Arthur treated me fairly. He lives his entire life around a football. Joseph agreed and nodded, but his response was not what Haley had hoped for. She anticipated that Joseph would begin to seek her once the barrier known as Arthur was gone. She was unaware that Joseph was not actively listening to her because he was so focused on getting his final marks and graduating. As he read a text book, it sort of drifted in and out of his mind.

Finally, he turned his head. I'm pleased you made up your mind regarding him before you ran off together, got hitched, and discovered that your life with him would be horrible if you didn't love him deeply enough.

He once more collected his thoughts. "You can and will improve without a doubt. You won't find the wrong man, and I don't think you're an airhead.

He didn't wait for a response before bending down to resume his reading.

Haley was perplexed. When she told Joseph the news about Arthur, she believed he would approach her right away and ask her out. She felt she understood the reclusive man from her time sitting and conversing with him, and she was able to assess his emotions. Was she interpreting their relationship based solely on her own reflected emotions? Could it be that she misread him? Was he reluctant to express his feelings for her because of his past experiences?

Haley was concerned that their relationship was coming to an end because they had been meeting at this coffee shop in the student union for some time to study together and just chat. I like you more as a buddy than anything else, you know. Nobody wants to hear those words from someone they are interested in romantically, male or female. Joseph was left to study while Haley got her books.

She went to Rose Waltz's dorm room, an old acquaintance of hers. She had known Rose well since elementary school. Haley and Rose were like sisters in contrast to the majority of their other close friends who had grown up, matured, and formed new friendships.

Even though Haley's black hair and Rose's dark brown hair were quite close in colour, they did not look that similar. Despite sharing a pair of brown eyes, they otherwise differed greatly. Rose was only five feet one inch taller than Haley, who stood at five feet five inches. Because she worked out and went jogging every day, Haley was slender and toned. Rose, though, had been energetic up until puberty. She then just let herself go, gaining weight till she was 180 pounds with wide hips and big, floppy tits. She was a little aggressive with people she had just met because she had not drawn a lot of attention due to her weight.

She was an authority on the other sex, just like many other people who have little to no relationship experience are. In high school, she had advised Haley repeatedly not to date Lukas and had only reluctantly stopped criticizing Arthur while Haley was seeing him. She was the ideal person to talk about Joseph because she had never even met him.

When Haley entered, she jumped into Rose's bed. They could talk for as long as they wanted because Rose's roommate was fortunately out for the evening. Rose was seated in her cozy office

CHAPTER 7

Chair at the computer desk. Rose majored in psychology, so it was easy for Haley to picture herself as her patient on the sofa and Rose as a practicing psychologist. Rose nearly wished she had glasses so she could look at her patient through them.

Why are you here on such a beautiful spring day?

Rose, Oh, God I'm at a loss on what to do. I am beginning to feel really deep feelings for Joseph, but he just doesn't seem that interested in me. I know that Arthur was just a college romance. What should I do?

Rose acknowledged that this was unusual male behavior. "At least he doesn't appear interested in you for the sake of a quick piece of ass, I suppose. Are you certain he isn't gay?

"I don't feel that way about him. Like Ambrose in high school, for example. Everyone was aware that he was in love with half the football squad, despite his denials.

Haley didn't express it, but she must have felt that Joseph was treating Rose the same way that all the boys appeared to treat Rose. You're a nice girl, but I don't want to have sex with you, is how I kind of felt. She didn't say it out loud, though. She was aware that Rose was dissatisfied with her own love life and angry that men didn't seem to be able to see past her size and the person inside.

The two decided that Haley should just put her relationship with Joseph on hold until he got his head out of his ass and realized what he wanted and needed. They continued their get-together and even had some fun criticizing guys in general.

When Haley failed to show up and sit with him before class, Joseph immediately noticed. She had been regularly studying with him before class. Both of them were focused on getting the most out of the educational system before entering the real world now that they were down to their final few classes before graduating. Haley felt confident in her place in life, but as she grew older, she began to take her education more seriously.

She was seated across from him on the opposite side of the room, Joseph saw as he looked up. He returned her smile as she raised her head to face him. She didn't appear to be angry with him, at least.

This continued for a few more days, or more precisely the week leading up to dead week and the occasionally frantic cramming for final examinations. After some time, Joseph stood up from his usual position and went over to her. "You've been missed. Why can't we continue to study together?

Haley acted as though she had to drudge herself away from her textbook. "Hello Joseph. I was totally absorbed by this paragraph. I believe the professor would especially focus on this subject in his essay questions, therefore I'm attempting to get as much information as I can from the passage.

"I am aware; I have been acting in a similar manner. In actuality, I wanted to know what your plans are for after graduation. Are you on vacation or a sabbatical of any kind?

"Well, my buddy Rose and I are preparing to spend a few weeks in my parents' cabin on the lake. We're going to relax, let our hair down, and simply take a break from everything. She will next do final interviews in a number of local school districts in her pursuit of a job as a school psychologist.

So, large gatherings on the lake?

She grinned at the idea. "Perhaps a couple, but not the entire two weeks. Would you like to visit the lake from up here?

It was now Joseph's time to grin. She didn't seem upset by his lack of interest during the last few weeks, based on the way she spoke. Contrary to what she thought, he was eager to propose to her but had been preoccupied with his finals. He was completely prepared to ask her to join him in his next chapter of life when school was over. "Yeah, after school is out, I'll have weekends off. Last but not least, no full-time job and full-time study. It will appear to be a vacation simply because I'll have time to myself because of this. I might even let free and drink a beer one evening soon.

Haley laughed at the idea of Joseph getting drunk with just one beer. They were once again pals once the ice had been shattered. Joseph was drawn to her. Now, she could see it. He was simply a person who could totally commit himself to finding a solution or achieving a goal when he was focused on doing so. His schooling was this objective. She would have to ascertain whether his next objective was her.

They engaged in a pleasant conversation before entering one of their final lessons together.

Graduation was finally approaching. To put on their gowns and caps, the approximately 2,000 graduates gathered in the field house. Rose Waltz, Haley, and Joseph gathered together so they would at least be aware of the whereabouts of the others following the wedding. In order to avoid being too near to one another during the event, they had to sit according to their areas of expertise in education. Nothing went wrong at all. The choir performing a few songs, the dull speeches about how the graduates were all future leaders with responsibilities, and then the never-ending line of people waiting to enter the platform to receive a simple folder containing a piece of paper explaining how to obtain the genuine diploma.

The entire process took more than three hours. The EMS team on standby responded to a few minor crises, particularly involving older families who had been seated for an excessive amount of time and some of them had developed health issues. Joseph hoped that none of the families from himself, Haley, or Rose were affected by the illness.

Gladly, everything went smoothly. After the many photos with family and friends, the three met back at the field house. A reception venue that Haley's parents had leased was going to be shared by the three at the last minute. In a minute, all of their families would move there. However, Joseph had a question for Haley before the three departed.

She was given his hands. She realized that they had never genuinely held hands before. I'm sorry to seem conceited, but might I present you to my family as my girlfriend? Haley

Haley gave him a short kiss on the lips because she was so delighted. They had their first kiss, she realized later. Although unmemorable, it was a beginning. She looked coyly at him. "I suppose you can, but only if I get to introduce you as my boyfriend," the speaker said.

She looked over at her friend and noticed the scowl on Rose's face. She shook her head at Rose and the scowl disappeared and a forced smile took its place. The trio quickly turned in their gowns and carted off their mortarboards and tassels as they headed to the reception. Haley hooked her arms with her best friend and her new boyfriend as they made their way through the crowd to the exit.

At the reception Joseph got to meet Haley's father, Brian Storm. Her mother had succumbed to cancer a few years ago and he was not yet looking to replace her. Brian was not a tall man at five foot eight inches in height but was a powerful force at 250 pounds of mostly muscle just now starting to become middle aged fat. He had started his first auto repair and tire shop when in his early 20's and now had two shops in this city and another two in nearby smaller communities. All were profitable.

Brian took an immediate liking to the slightly taller young man. He could see that Joseph was a person after his own blood, a hard working and focused mature young man at twenty-three. He also remembered Joseph playing football for the university.

CHAPTER 8

Joseph also immediately liked Haley's father. He could see that this man appreciated honesty and hard work. Heck he even had a little grease under his fingernails. He seemed to be an average mechanic, not the owner of several successful businesses. There was power in his handshake but it was controlled. Brian didn't feel the need to play power games with this young man.

Haley got to meet Joseph's parents and grandparents. His father, Martha, was your average looking business man. At fifty years of age he was now grey haired but out of shape with a protruding gut. Joseph's mother, Peyton, complemented her husband. At forty-eight years of age she was also going grey without trying to hide or highlight her longish hair. She was matronly looking and unfortunately overweight like her husband. Both, though, seemed full of life and were immediately accepting Haley into the family. Joseph's grandparents were likewise welcoming and quick to welcome Joseph's new girlfriend into the family.

Joseph's family had been forced to travel about a hundred miles from his hometown to the graduation. Not as bad as some families but not as local as Haley's family. Unfortunately his older sister and brother lived a lot farther away and were unable to attend his graduation.

The two didn't have much time to celebrate their new relationship as many friends, and for Haley in particular, many family came to celebrate their accomplishments. Rose and her family also deserved attention from the others and for all it became a confusing mass of people. Rose did remember when introduced his old friend, Jamie Brown, who was now living here in their university town. Jamie was a draftsman for a construction company and making a good wage with only a community college education.

Rose followed Jamie with her eyes as he greeted old acquaintances that were members of Joseph's family. Jamie had been treated as a member of the family as the boys were growing up. Jamie was taller than Joseph at six foot even and had kept himself in shape with jogging and doing MMA with Joseph.

What Rose didn't notice was that Jamie had been a little smitten with her also but was not comfortable with the thought of getting to know an overweight girl. That was just wrong in today's thinking of every guy should be dating the princess of the class, not the frog. He tried to not notice her as she greeted her friends and family after their introduction.

Thus began their relationship.

The new couple went out on their first real date a couple of evenings later. Joseph had been in a small apartment while in college but now opted for a bigger one since he had a promotion and wage increase from the clothing store, The Brass Lamp. No one really could say where the name came from but it was a successful endeavor and Joseph was intent on making every opportunity pay off.

He moved in a matter of days since his old apartment had come mostly furnished and he only had his clothes, bicycle, TV, game system, and laptop to move to the new place. Of course Haley wanted to help and did so. She found by looking that he preferred briefs to boxers.

Their first date was to a nice but not too pretentious Italian restaurant. Haley had been there many times with her family and was well known. The proprietor sat them in a great spot and service was excellent. Over the wine and pasta they talked and found more about each other. For instance Joseph was decidedly conservative in his outlook in life and with his money while Haley was a little more liberal both with her thinking and her money. She didn't mind paying taxes while Joseph was dead set against giving money to politicians who seemed to just waste any money coming their way while telling all and sundry that they had better idea for the use of money than the taxpayer. They had a good spirited talk on that subject.

After supper they went for a walk around the downtown area and Joseph told Haley about his job. Haley related that she was going to work on her dad to increase his advertising so the business could grow some more. Maybe he would even look at Joseph's home town in the near future.

After the walk it was time to say goodnight as both needed to be up in the morning. Joseph delivered Haley to her father's home and they stood kissing on the front stoop for a while. They enjoyed their interlude and were not looking forward to being apart for a few days.

CHAPTER 9

The trip to the lake was a great vacation for Haley and Rose. They got to act as though they were still in high school and have a great time without adult worries. Neither was looking for one-night stands though Rose did comment once or twice how nice it would be to have a zipless fuck. Both got a good laugh out of that. Joseph came up on the first weekend and hung out on the beach with them both. Rose actually smiled at some of Joseph's stories about life in retail.

Things were looking up for the twosome. Haley was quick to do anything her dad needed in the shop and even took over doing day trips to the other stores to make sure everything was running smoothly. She knew that he would be resistant to some of her changes, especially if that change involved spending money, so she started slowly by setting up accounts on social media and getting signage informing the public at each store. As these ideas took off and customers liked what she had done then she suggested other marketing ideas to help build the business.

Towards the end of the year one of her ideas was to take beefcake shots of some of the mechanics for a calendar. She posed the idea to her dad as a take off of the old cheesecake calendars that had graced repair shops and tool chests for years before political correctness had forced them to be removed. She reasoned that a large percentage of their clientele were women and they would love to see a picture of their favorite mechanic in action for a month.

Brian reluctantly agreed and the shoot was on.

Joseph and Haley continued to date at least three nights a week. They would usually go out for a meal, maybe catch a movie and then head home. Haley found her own apartment and had moved out of her father's place. It was larger than Joseph's apartment since her dad was still helping with living expenses, just not as much as when she was in school.

They also went out with groups of friends on the weekends. These groups included Rose and, on occasion, Jamie. Jamie did date some other women but didn't bring any ever if Rose was going to be in the group. He didn't really stop to wonder why but he instinctively felt it would be wrong to throw a relationship with another woman in Rose's face.

During these group outings Rose and Jamie seemed to automatically drift to each other and were always deep in conversation with each other to everyone else's amusement. Joseph would tease Jamie when they were alone about his having multiple girlfriends, you know, any other woman and Rose. Jamie would get red in the face and very defensive and deny that he was in any way attracted to Rose. She was just a friend, yada, yada, yada. Joseph would just laugh at him.

Haley never brought up Jamie when talking to Rose. Rose did that often enough as it was. She was trying to keep a level head where Jamie was concerned but she knew what she wanted and cried when she decided that Jamie wasn't that interested in her.

Of all things that could be a point of real contention, the relationship between Jamie and Rose was actually the one that caused the most serious arguments between Haley and Joseph. Haley wanted Jamie to either declare his interest in Rose or not be part of the group outings any more. Joseph wanted to stay out of their relationship and let them figure it out.

Some of their movie nights descended into long conversations about how Rose was hurting and her ego was too fragile to accept rejection by Jamie. Joseph would counter that Jamie was obviously not mature enough to enter into a relationship with Rose if he had any qualms about her weight. The only thing the couple could agree on was that Jamie and Rose were attracted to each other and would make a great pair.

As most serious relationships go Joseph and Haley's evolved into one that included a physical relationship.

One night, a Saturday night by chance, they had gone out with a large group for bowling and beer. Rose and Jamie seemed to have come to an agreement and the rest of the group actually sat open-mouthed as Jamie asked Rose for a date. Haley was then so overcome that she immediately attacked Joseph and left him breathless. Since the date proposal came at the end of the evening the group soon broke up and all left for their respective homes. Jamie and Rose went off together to the nearest Denny's for a midnight snack and more discussion of their new relationship.

CHAPTER 10

Haley got into Joseph's car and turned to him. "Take me home to your apartment stud and make me scream."

Joseph leaned over and kissed her hard. Their tongues dueled for a few moments before he cupped her breast and gently squeezed. He pulled back a little. "Do you want hard and nasty or soft and gentle?"

She smiled her little sexy smile. "Maybe a little of both. Why don't we explore and find out what works best?"

He nodded and soon they were at his apartment. While driving he noticed that Haley was unbuttoning the top few buttons of her blouse exposing her nice cleavage. She was also caressing his cock through his jeans whenever he had to stop for a traffic light or stop sign.

At his apartment building they raced up the stairs to his apartment on the second floor. Haley was rubbing his back and grabbing his buttocks as he fumbled getting his key in the door. Instead of being frustrated he was smiling. He wanted her and obviously she wanted him.

Finally the key found its way into the lock and they were in the room. Later he wondered if he left the key in the lock but somehow he had managed to get it back into his pocket before he and Haley had tried to undress the other simultaneously. Later they both agreed the comedy of them trying to undress each other in such a furious and quick manner might have gotten them prize money if it had been videoed.

Finally Joseph had Haley's blouse and bra off and she had his shirt off and his jeans unbuttoned and the fly down before they managed to get enough control so they could finish the job. Joseph knelt down on the floor and pulled Haley's slacks down exposing her tiny bikini panties. No, they weren't some lace under thing, just pretty cotton panties that hid her treasure spot. He kissed her legs and then her lower abdomen before kissing her mons and actually tried to lick her pussy with her legs closed and her panties still in place. Even though she couldn't feel much in the spot she wanted him she gave out a small moan and held his face against her crotch.

Finally she was able to lean on him as she kicked off the slacks. This then allowed Joseph to finish making her nude in front of him. He slowly drew down the last garment protecting her, noticing at the same time, that the gusset was wet from her arousal. Her scent was natural, enticing, and made his cock throb in his jeans.

He couldn't resist. As soon as her panties were off he dove back into her center. He was kissing and licking for all he was worth and she definitely appreciated it. She squealed and moaned and caressed his head while telling him how much she loved him.

Soon her legs were shaking and shuddering from the orgasmic sensations engendered by his tongue and ardor.

Before she could collapse he stood quickly and picked her up and carried her to the bedroom and deposited her there gently before ripping his remaining clothes off.

His six inch cock was hard and throbbing. The precum was smeared around the head from being in his briefs for so long. Haley watched with approval at the sight of his bobbing cock as he kicked his briefs away. She smiled up at him and spread her legs and extended her arms in invitation. He accepted and moved between her outspread legs and centered his cock on her hot cauldron and was soon fully imbedded in her velvety pussy.

Her legs wrapped around his hips and pulled him in tight as her arms clutched his shoulders. As his first stroke bottomed out as deep as he could go she raised up and kissed him hard. "Oh god, I have waited so long for this. Fuck me, Baby, fuck me hard."

Joseph did just that. Even though the feeling of her beautiful vagina wanted him to explode since it had been a very long time since he had participated in a sexual act other than masturbation he tried to control his urge to immediately impregnate this female. The age old dance began.

He thrust hard and she responded with her own pelvic lift and ready acceptance and welcoming of his powerful stroke. She and he both grunted with the exertion. His pelvic bone smashed into her clit over and over again and she made sure her pelvis was tilted up enough to take the full impact of his thrust. She chanted over and over about how much she loved his cock and how she had wanted his body over hers. This drove him to slam harder into her. He started to sweat and drops began forming on his face, finally migrating to his nose and jaw to fall on her face. Instead of being turned off she opened her mouth and accepted each drop of his sweat as though it was manna from heaven. She then smiled lasciviously at him and begged for more.

Soon though rational thought was driven from her head as she laid her head back and cried out her satisfaction in the first climax induced by her new and hopefully last lover. She shook and jerked and clutched at his shoulders as her feet beat a tattoo on his buttocks. Nothing before prepared her for the pleasure of sex with the man she could spend the rest of her life with.

Her orgasm caused her already snug pussy to spasm around his nicely sized cock and actually grab him hard enough to stop his thrusts for a short bit of time. When she loosened up again he was able to start thrusting again. Now, though, the thrusting was gentler and more loving, not just hard sexual banging of her pussy. Haley pulled up and kissed him again. This time longer and more loving.

"Thank you for that orgasm. It has to be the most intense one I have ever felt. I know the next one will be slower and last longer. You are the best, Joseph. Now love me some more."

They changed position. It was a first for Haley to be on top. It was a strange position so she took her time to get her knees right and then to slowly move up and down on Joseph's raging cock. She also rubbed her pelvis against his when he was fully imbedded. She didn't know if he was getting much from this but the feelings for her were fantastic. She was in control. She was setting the tempo. She posted up and down and forward and back as she felt the need.

Soon she was shaking and couldn't quite get over the top but Joseph was thrusting up into her as he could. She whimpered her need and frustration but when he added a lone finger into her cleft and she could now rub against something hard again. Her cries were not of frustration suddenly. She was suddenly at the peak and sliding over the edge. Her body was stiff then pliant. Her screams of pleasure were cut off suddenly and then on again. She was perspiring freely making their bodies slick.

As she came down from her second orgasm Haley collapsed onto Joseph's chest. This brought her pelvis up slightly so he could thrust up and now his orgasm was coming and coming rapidly. "In me, in me, please." Now he knew she wanted his sperm inside her accepting pussy and not on his belly. He groaned and started to shoot. "I feel it. I feel it! Oh good, I feel you shooting in me."

Haley actually had a small quite satisfying orgasm just from feeling her man shoot inside her.

They then both collapsed. Joseph was limp with Haley lying on his body, covering him. They didn't move when his wilted sword fell out of her. They didn't move when a gush of his sperm came out of her pussy but Haley did giggle a little. They finally moved when their bodies cooled enough to need a cover. Haley snuggled in Joseph's arms and drifted off to sleep. Both were content and happy.

This now set the stage for their relationship going forward. Haley was becoming more important to her dad's business with her ideas to help market the business more. Joseph was taking on more responsibilities at work and taking a couple of classes a semester for his masters' in business. They survived Black Friday that year. Joseph was at work from 1:00 a.m. until 10:00 that night with only a crappy sandwich for sustenance. He fell into bed and slept until forced up on Saturday morning to go and open the store for the weekend sales that weren't much different than the Black Friday deals. Haley didn't see him until late Sunday night.

They had supper together and then made love until Joseph fell asleep.

They continued to date. They had small arguments and didn't speak to each other for a couple of days. During this time Rose and Jamie went hot and warm but never cold. Whenever they were in a warm period of just friends Rose's self-esteem would tank and she would speak nasty thoughts to Haley about both Jamie and Joseph. Even though Haley claimed that nothing Rose would say could hurt her feelings about Joseph there would be niggling little suspicions left there.

Rose would talk about how Jamie was fickle and never would commit to the relationship. She would then wonder aloud if Joseph suffered from the same affliction. Other times Rose would be angry and talk about asshole men who just wanted the milk free and not ready to buy the cow. As time went by these comments got more pointed and heated whenever Jamie didn't show the love that Rose craved. Joseph was just tarred by the same brush. Truth be known but Rose was jealous of Joseph and Haley's solid relationship.

Joseph's public lack of affections toward Haley didn't help. She wanted her man to walk with his arm around her and rub elbows with her when they dined out but Joseph would hold hands will strolling and insisted on sitting across from Haley when dining so he could see her face.

Their lovemaking was intense though and something to grab onto. Joseph also seemed to be exclusive as was Haley. They discussed moving in together but Haley felt her father would be terribly disappointed in her even though he liked Joseph.

Joseph, though, since he had been burned by fickle females before was loath to discuss marriage with Haley. Haley stayed away from the subject since Joseph didn't seem to want to discuss their future. They coasted along for quite a while even when both families would ask each one privately about when nuptials could be planned. Haley would just state that she was willing to wait on Joseph. Joseph would just shrug his shoulders and change the subject.

Finally Joseph decided it was time to pull the trigger. He had saved enough to put a good down payment on a house and had purchased a ring. Haley's twenty-fifth birthday was coming up and all of the family was planning a big birthday celebration at a local restaurant. Joseph felt it would be the perfect backdrop for a proposal followed by a short engagement and then wedding. Haley could go on the hunt for a house for them both and they would be set for marital bliss.

CHAPTER 11

He wanted it to be a complete surprise so he didn't even talk with Jamie about it. He figured Jamie and Rose were on their hot cycle again and Jamie would spill the beans to Rose and then Rose would have to clue Haley in.

It was the complete surprise that he intended. The stack of presents was high and Haley was in the process of opening each and every one. She would stop and exclaim with each and then thank the giver. Occasionally she would have to look the gift in confusion until someone would explain what the hell it actually was. Then her delighted laugh would ring out as she thanked the giver again. Finally there was none left and she knew that Joseph had not given her a present. Maybe it would be an all night of great sex. She was smiling at him when he knelt in front of her. "Haley, my love, I would like to ask you a simple question." He pulled the ring box from behind his back and opened it. "Would you do the honor of marrying me?"

Her face fell. She was thinking that it couldn't be true, not today of all days. Rose couldn't be right could she? What she didn't realize was that some of her thoughts were being expressed out loud. "No, not today. Why are you asking today of all days? I can't believe it but it must be true." She was shaking her head as tears started to fall but they were not the tears of happiness.

Joseph was speechless. Here he had spent so much time with Haley. They had dated, made love, and planned for a future and she was shaking her head negatively. Here in front of family and friends she was refusing him without an answer as to why.

He had never felt so used or betrayed. He stood and walked out of the venue and caught a cab to the closest bar to his apartment. It was time to get stinking drunk. It was a promise to himself that was easy to keep. As he seldom drank he was able to get plowed in a short time. From that point on it was just a matter of maintaining the illusion of being in control. His attitude guaranteed that he was left alone at the end of the bar for the evening.

When the bar finally closed he staggered out into the summer night. He was still trying to make some kind of plans for his future. The future he had foreseen was now just ashes that needed swept aside for the new future. Since this wasn't his hometown he could see moving somewhere far away to cleanse himself of anything that would remind him of Haley.

In his stupor he wandered the wrong way towards his apartment. He was actually headed for the large park nearby. He stumbled and fell a couple of times but got up and continued his errant way into the park. There was a center part of the park that was overgrown brush and scrub trees. The city let it stay wild since the terrain didn't lend itself to any other use. Joseph was feeling a little chilled as the night air cooled so when he made it to the brush he dropped and crawled in like a wounded wild animal.

When he woke the sun was high in the sky. His head hurt. Well, actually it felt like it was trying to fall off his neck. The throbbing in tune with his heartbeat felt like a bass drum and he wasn't able to hear anything over the beat in his ears. The light hurt his eyes so he kept them shut. It had been a long time since he had been hung over but, as he remembered what had happened the night before, it wasn't going to be the last time. He groaned as he rolled over in his brush bed. He was nauseated also and didn't think he could stand up.

He finally put his arm over his face to make it a little darker and barely opened his eyes. He sure wasn't at his apartment. He was completely baffled as to where he was. Had he driven out of the city? It wasn't that large a city so he could be near the river. He knee and elbow crawled out where the sun was more intense and not filtered by the leafy brush. His vision was still hampered by the brightness but he could now hear kids playing. He finally figured he was at the park. He wanted to shake his head in disgust at how drunk he had been but his head still felt like it would fall off his neck.

He kept his head down as he made his way to a more familiar area and then was finally pointed toward his apartment.

Since it had been a Tuesday when Haley's party had been planned for, the actual day of her birth anniversary, it had to be Wednesday. He stopped to rest at a bench on the edge of the park. He had to think. He checked his phone and found it was dead. He was late to work and needed to call in. A few feet away was a lone pay phone, one of the few still in existence. He made his way there and found enough coins to make the ancient machine work. Now he had to remember the store phone number but he could only remember the number of the headquarters. He shrugged his shoulders and placed the call.

Circumstances conspired to put his vague thoughts into action. Instead of just calling in sick he now was talking to the main switchboard. He had the operator first call the store and inform them he was ill, then put him through to his regional manager. A few minutes of discussion was all it took to set in motion his exit from his current city. He asked for the chance to go to a poor performing store as far away as possible to start over. If he could make a poor performer do better it would also help his standing in the company. He asked for an immediate transfer after explaining his reason for going.

Thankfully his district manager had a store in mind and it needed immediate help. There were a couple of supervisors that could handle Joseph's load here locally for a short bit while his replacement was being groomed. Joseph would have to hit the ground running on the store in mind as its performance was so poor that discussions had begun to close the store and move the merchandise to other stores.

Joseph hung up and made his way to his apartment. He figured Jamie would be looking for him but he didn't want to see or talk to anybody today.

His lease had been up for some time so he was just renting month to month. He would just let his landlord know of his leaving and give up his damage deposit in lieu of having to give notice to move.

At his apartment there was a note on the door. Jamie had been there looking for him. Joseph left the note in place. He would talk to Jamie but when he was ready.

After a shower, shave and a small breakfast along with a pain killer, he felt somewhat human. He called for a moving company to come and give him a quote on storing his belongings until he found a place to stay in his new city.

It must have been a slow day as a representative showed up within an hour to discuss options. Joseph was intending to drive his car loaded with staples and clothes, just enough to get established. The rest of stuff would then be trucked to him when he needed it. The rep was surprised that Joseph wanted the movers there as soon as possible. Joseph just explained that the opportunity for advancement had suddenly appeared and his employer wanted him to move immediately. The movers would be there the next morning. The rep and Joseph shook hands and Joseph got busy sorting his stuff. His plan was to be on the road by the next night. Clothes were sorted according to business need, a little casual clothing, and seasonal need. He packed his coffee maker, his microwave, and some pans, plates and utensils that would go into his trunk. His flat screen was too large to go into the car so he intended to use his desktop monitor as a TV for a short while. That meant his computer had to be packed. Soon he had a car full of stuff ready to be packed.

CHAPTER 12

He stopped and looked around. It was now after 5:00 and he was getting hungry. He had charged his phone but had neglected to turn it back on. When he did so he found his mailbox was full of voice mails and he had literally hundreds of text messages. Most were on the order of "Where are you? We need to talk." He deleted all but the few from his employees who had been told that he was abruptly leaving.

He answered those with a short message that the opportunity to show what he could do with a bad performer was too good to pass up but that he needed to move quickly in order to get to work as there was a limited time to improve the store before it was deemed too poor to stay open. He wished them all well.

Joseph went back to the bar where he had gotten drunk the night before. It was so foreign for him to ever drink that he didn't think he would be disturbed there. He ate a specialty of the grill and had a couple of beers but stayed sober this night.

His phone went off a couple of times. Once was Haley, another was his dad, once from Rose and one from Jamie. He called and talked to his dad for a bit. He didn't dwell on the proposal at all and deflected any questions about the humiliation brought on by a public refusal of his proposal. He just told his dad he was moving immediately due to the sudden opportunity to increase his worth to the company.

After talking to his dad he texted Jamie and just told him he would talk with him the next day and that he was tremendously busy right now.

As he sat and contemplated his move he mentally tried to determine if there was anything of worth at Haley's apartment. He decided that anything he had left there she could donate to charity. As for anything she had left at his apartment he would have it delivered to her apartment.

When he got back to the apartment he found another note on the door. It was from Haley begging him to call her. He really couldn't understand how or why she would want to talk to him after dumping his ass the night before. He was too tired to even contemplate about having the energy to talk to her and didn't think there was any reason to discuss anything with her.

He undressed and crawled into bed. He was too tired to even dream. When he woke in the morning there was someone pounding on his door. At least he hoped it was someone pounding on his door as he had a headache from the few beers consumed the night before. Then he could hear the doorknob rattling. He had set the deadbolt the night before and there was no key for it. He usually only locked the door knob itself but Haley had a key to that and he didn't want to hear her or see her so he had hit the deadbolt.

After a few minutes whoever was at the door must have decided to give up and leave. Joseph didn't care enough to even look out the window to see someone leave. He didn't want to hear explanations or get reassurances from Haley or anyone who might represent her. Her message had been plain enough, she didn't love him enough to marry him. Maybe she was waiting for Arthur. Maybe Arthur was already in contact and soon to arrive here. Joseph concluded he was just a diversion until her real love could appear.

The movers showed up at 10:00. They were very professional. The items he was going to take with him were quickly moved to the side and the men packed his other things into a truck and it was gone to a storage facility owned by the moving company. He signed the contract outlining rents and penalties and gave it to the foreman before he left for his next job.

Now Joseph just needed to get his stuff to the car. First he called a cab to take him back to the restaurant where his car was parked. There were numerous post-it notes on the windshield. He pulled them all off without reading a single one and balled them up and dropped them in the nearest trash can before driving back to his apartment. Luckily he had been gone long enough for someone to leave another note on his door. He didn't bother to read it or even take it down.

He called his landlord and told him the apartment was vacant and ready to be cleaned and shown. His landlord was sorry to see him go as he had been an excellent tenant but wished him well.

Now for the final visit. He headed for Jamie's place. He figured Jamie would be home and alone. He was half right.

Jamie had company. Joseph assumed it was Rose but didn't really care. After Jamie answered the door and then gave the surprised Joseph a huge hug he asked Joseph to come in but Joseph caught a glimpse of someone behind Jamie and turned his invitation down. He instead asked Jamie to come out to his car for a few moments.

Jamie went back inside and spoke to his guest for a few minutes. Joseph figured that if the guest was Rose he had about twenty minutes before Haley arrived. He was intending to be long gone before that time. He didn't want to get drunk again tonight.

Jamie joined him at the hood of his car. Jamie could see that it was packed. Joseph just informed him that he was moving but not where to. Jamie tried to get Joseph to talk with Haley.

"Joseph, you don't know what happened after you left the party. Haley's dad came over and wanted to know what was going on. She told him that since you asked her to marry her on her twenty-fifth birthday that you must be only wanting her inheritance. Brian wanted to know how you knew about the trust fund from her grandmother. No one could answer him. When he kept asking her she became less and less sure that you were some kind of gold-digger and started to cry."

He stopped for a second. "Did you know about the trust fund and that she was to get control of it on her twenty-fifth birthday?"

Joseph shook his head in denial. What a shit storm. Money almost always caused more trouble than it was worth.

"Yeah, I thought so. Anyhow Rose and I have been arguing for the last two days about it. She is adamant that you knew about the inheritance and that was why you picked her birthday to ask her to marry you."

Joseph shook his head again. "What have I ever done to her?"

Jamie shrugged his shoulders. "I suppose it is really my fault. I love her and I can't stay away from her but I am embarrassed by her weight. I wish I could get over it but I can't. I think that she is so upset by me that she has been talking against you to Haley. It's the only plausible explanation."

Joseph stood up. "Well, it that was all it took then this is all for the best. She would never be happy as she would always be looking for ways that I was not the man she wanted or needed. She can have Rose and be happy knowing the gold-digger is gone. Now she can be looking for the next one. Maybe not being you or me or in any way associated with us will let Rose approve of him, whoever he is."

He turned to get into the car. He turned around and tossed the ring box to Jamie. "Why don't you grow up a little more and realize you love her and can't live without her? You need her and obviously she loves you and needs you. Have the damned ring resized if necessary and give it to her."

Jamie tried to get him to stop but Joseph was done talking. He got into the car and backed out and was soon gone down the street.

When Haley arrived she found Jamie still standing alone holding the ring box.

CHAPTER 13

Joseph deliberately did not tell Jamie where he was headed. He had also asked his company to not let anyone not associated with the company know where he was going. He didn't even tell his parents or siblings.

He soon found living accommodations. It was a small apartment, just about the size of his last one. As the new assistant manager he should have a bigger place but he didn't need the space. He arranged for the movers to bring his other belongings and household goods.

His first day of work was enlightening. He met the store manager and the man showed him a letter from the home office. The manager was to keep his title but Joseph had a free hand to make changes as he saw fit. There would be a united front from the two but if the manager tried in any way to thwart Joseph then the manager, Austin Eddy, would be the first to go.

Joseph told Austin that he was sorry that the head office was taking this stance. It was not his intention to undermine the existing leadership, just help it.

He asked Austin to not announce his presence just yet. He wanted to anonymously observe the staff for a few days. He might be able to get a handle on the problems quicker if he was an unknown.

He then went out and came in the front of the store. It was located in a busy mall and in a good central location. The merchandise was the best of the company and the store manikins were dressed appropriately. The population of the city was about two times that of the college town that Joseph had come from. It meant a larger potential customer base but also more competition. The reasons for the store's failure had to be found and quickly.

He entered the store and perused the racks. No employee approached to ask if he or she could help. That needed addressed. Customers needed to see that someone was ready and willing to help if necessary.

Then he observed the real problem. A couple of black girls came in and were immediately accosted and encouraged to take their business elsewhere. This happened again and again and not only with black customers. Asian, Muslim, Indian, Jamaican, Hispanic were all treated the same. Joseph sent off a text to the home office for someone to come and provide diversity training. He also observed that only white employees were visible at any time.

After a few days of observation at various times that the store was open he had developed a plan of action.

First he had Austin introduce him as the new assistant manager. After the introductions he quickly let the entire staff know what their financial position was. He didn't sugar coat anything. He laid out that the store had been losing money steadily for some time and was slated to be closed unless there was an immediately turn around.

He then went into an analysis of why there were poor sales in this market. He discussed the competition and how they all had to work to compete with other similar stores and even with Wal-Mart and Target, stores that most didn't feel were competitors for the clothing market.

Finally he laid out a plan of action to help guide all employees in their mission to save the store. He challenged them to think about the bottom line at all times. Theft and waste were part of any equation so he addressed those issues also.

As he looked out at the staff he could see that a few agreed with him but others had already shut him down in their minds. They were only there for the paycheck and not much else. Since he had already identified some staff who needed to be let go it didn't surprise him that those were the staff members who were already showing their inability to help the problem.

He had their employment jackets and intended to sit down with each of them this morning. After he spoke his intention to talk to each employee was announced. He also let each one know that he was open to ideas to help increase business. He had found already that employees who were close to the customers had good ideas on how to grow a business.

The morning went fast. He spoke with employees on an alphabetical basis. That way it could not look like he was cutting dead weight first. He hated to let anyone go but this was needed to help make the store more palatable to those whom had been mistreated when trying to buy clothing from his store.

He told each employee that the corporate office was sending additional help. They weren't alone in wanting to keep their jobs. Extra resources would help. The diversity training team was slated to arrive in a few days and money for additional ad campaigns was being approved. The PR and marketing departments were fast tracking new ads. A little of the next season's apparel line was also being shipped.

At the end of the first day he needed eight new employees. Since that left holes in the schedule Joseph was going to have to work the sales floor a lot more than anticipated. Since this wasn't a new experience for him, he felt he could do this. He just needed more help.

The next morning he was dressed in his best clothes purchased through the company. Instead of a suit and tie he wanted to project the image of what the store's clothing could look on the average person.

He had a quick team meeting before the doors were unlocked. He stressed service to all potential customers regardless of their race or creed.

Things picked up immediately. A lone Muslim woman came in with her head covered. Joseph was thankful that she didn't have her face covered also. Joseph met her at the front of the store and was soon engaging her in a conversation about what her needs and wants were. As expected she wanted something a little daring but still keeping with her religious beliefs. As a team they found some clothing and scarves that would fit the bill.

This set the bar for the other staff members. Helping customers find what they wanted became the norm instead of the unusual. The store had its first profitable day in a couple of years.

CHAPTER 15

Joseph was working fifteen to eighteen hours a day, seven days a week. Instead of being tired and worn out it actually energized him. No, it was those hours alone in his apartment that gave him the most stress. When he was exhausted by work he didn't think of his abortion of a relationship with Haley.

He didn't try to date. It took too much effort to even think about dating or even meeting a new love interest. He would lock up the store after restocking and cleaning, yes they had stopped the cleaning contract for a while to save money, and go find a small meal to eat. He would then have a beer or two before showering and dropping into bed.

He would wake at about seven each morning so he could be at the store by eight. They didn't open until ten, when all the rest of the mall opened, but there was paperwork, interviews, product to receive, and phone calls to make. He was busy right up till opening.

The store improved during the course of four months.

Due to his commitment, he obtained two pay raises during that time. Bonuses were also received by his workers. These incentives were greatly valued because they had been hard to come by over the previous few years. He still needed to teach some new hires, but he knew which individuals already on the team could do it. Although Joseph wasn't as needed on the sales floor, he still made an effort to drop by and assist one or two customers every day.

Austin took the message and made sure he was ready to assist when it was required.

Joseph had more time to himself as a result of the higher sales and decreased necessity for him to work. To wear himself out, he tried to exercise as frequently as he could. Even when he wasn't fatigued, his sleep was frequently interrupted. He would experience nightmares in which Arthur, Rose, Jamie, and Haley teased and mocked him.

He couldn't go back to sleep once he woke up crying out Haley's name. He finally saw a doctor and obtained a sleep medication to aid in his rest. Though he detested doing it, he had to rest. He would take long strolls, but that simply gave him more time to consider Haley and what she might be up to by this point. Hell, she could even be married to Arthur already.

Once a week, Joseph would give his folks a call to catch up on family events. He still hadn't given them his whereabouts. He didn't really understand why, as he thought Haley had either rekindled her relationship with Arthur or was starting a new one, but something urged him not to tell them where he was at just yet. His mother made a few attempts to bring up Haley, but Joseph always cut her off. He was still hurt by the way she rejected him at her birthday party. Finally, Joseph had to warn her that if she continued to bring up Haley, he would stop calling. Even though his mother was quite disappointed, she agreed to keep her silence.

Joseph sent Jamie several texts. After moving, he received a new phone number. Additionally, he informed Jamie that he would break off contact with him if Jamie ever tried to bring up Haley or if Haley managed to obtain Joseph's new phone number. He tried to convince himself that Haley wouldn't try to get in touch with him, but he couldn't. In his worst moments, he saw Haley grabbing hold of him to force a new romance upon him.

Joseph tried the date game again with little success now that he had some free time. Every date was tainted by his mistrust of a woman's motivations. He began to wonder if his date had already moved on to the next man in her life the moment a discussion become Lukewarm. Rarely did he take the same woman on more than two dates.

He increased his drinking. He would consume a 12-pack on his weekends off while moping around by himself in his apartment. It wasn't enough to erase the memory, but it was enough to deepen his melancholy and sustain his sense of inadequacy. Even though he was engaging in self-destructive activity, he didn't care.

He was requested to transfer to another underperforming store after posting six consecutive months of earnings in the first one. He relocated once more, this time to a new city two states away. He reiterated his evaluation of the operations. However, he didn't notice any racial bias here and the personnel appeared to want to assist clients. No, something else was going on in this situation. It would require more research.

The store manager actively opposed him as well. Bridget Cummings was the female in question. She was divorced, middle-aged, and had a few college-age children. Joseph politely rejected her attempts when she first tried to seduce him, citing their professional connection. She then instructed personnel to disregard Joseph's advice.

After several months of looking, Joseph eventually discovered a clue after a lot of investigation. Regular invoices were being sent to corporate by the cleaning firm and the office supply store, both small, locally owned businesses, but they weren't quite in line with the agreed-upon costs. He reported his worries to corporate for additional research.

After a month, Bridget was abruptly let go. It was discovered that Bridget was receiving kickbacks from the cleaning service and the office supply business while they were billing extra. This information only partially explained the losses, but after Bridget was fired, the revenues returned to the levels that were anticipated. They were never able to establish that she was also skimming anyplace else.

Another store asked a new manager named Joseph to come in and help increase sales. He was developing a reputation as the go-to person for solving issues.

Thus, Joseph's life's subsequent chapter began. He was anticipated to discover issues in numerous stores within four to six months. Some were obvious, like the first store, and required new people as well as a change in customer service philosophy to resolve. Others were hazy and concerned both inventory and monetary thefts. Sometimes it took longer to resolve these, but finally the thefts were under control. A small number of employees were abruptly laid off, while another group also had legal issues with the police. Joseph shook his head at the idea that while an employee who stole only a few hundred dollars was given over to the police, an executive who stole thousands would simply be fired.

He was doing his online master's degree at a prominent university at this time. When he graduated, his compensation was significantly increased.

His social life slightly improved. In fact, he invited some women out on three or four occasions before he dumped them. They actually went on ten dates until Joseph seemed to lose interest and broke up the burgeoning romance. Sometimes the lack of spark is the only reason. Other times, a spark of attraction and compatibility would appear, but something else would take place. He frequently discovered that the woman shared her sexual activity with others. For him, this was a deal-breaker right away. At the age of twenty-seven, he wasn't expecting to find a virgin, but he at least hoped she wasn't being used as a playground.

The problem of trust persisted. The nightmares of Haley, Arthur, Rose, and Jamie would recur whenever he began to get close to a new love interest. He could hear people making fun of his credulity. He would break up with her after a few evenings like that. Naturally, he always let them down by telling them that the fault was with him and not with them.

Every now and then, Jamie would text him to inquire when he was coming back to visit. Joseph disregarded them. He didn't have a cause to return. He was not a member of the alumni group and had never heard from those considerate people. He reasoned that his mailing address was too likely to change for them.

Joseph received a text message from Jamie informing him that Rose and he were getting married and that Joseph would be the best man. Considering Haley to be the maid of honor, Joseph declined. His kind present was given without a return address.

Joseph did visit his family's festivities at home. His parents honored his request to keep Haley off the subject. His siblings actually had no queries or comments because they hadn't met her. Before the first family meeting, Joseph's mother spoke softly to ensure that neither his brother nor sister said anything.

Joseph showed his young nieces and nephews a lot of love. He made full use of the uncle card. To each occasion, he brought pricey gifts and made sure to take everyone out at least once for ice cream and candy. It was fortunate that he like children's films because they insisted that he take them to as many showings at the neighborhood theater as possible.

The fact that Joseph needed to show such love to his nieces and nephews but didn't have any of his own and didn't seem interested in any lady enough to rectify that situation upset Joseph's parents. Following the previous family reunion, Joseph went back to his most recent job. Before making a move, he was tying up a few last loose ends. He was already looking forward to what he would discover. At least now, the most of the problems were minor and consisted just of manager suggestions for improvements that would have a beneficial impact on the bottom line. He had rejected calls from corporate to go back to the headquarters and take on those responsibilities. Instead of going back to the scene of his own failure, Joseph was really considering switching careers and returning to school. His superiors were unaware of the reasons behind his adamant opposition to a promotion and a move back to the business headquarters because he had never explained why he wanted the change in settings. Even after a site visit, Joseph's manager was unable to fully understand why he would not even go to the home office.

But this day was distinct. Instead of management visiting him, a recognizable but unwelcome visage entered his frame of vision. In order to clear his brain, Joseph had taken a brief break from his final paperwork to walk out onto the sales floor. Out of the corner of his eye, he noticed a familiar face while assisting a customer. It is impossible. He averted his gaze. He was able to complete helping the customer by focusing.

He turned back after the customer left for the cashier but failed to spot her. Possibly, it was simply someone who looked like Haley. Outside of The Brass Lamp's highest management, nobody knew where he was, so it must have been, he reasoned.

He turned to return to the tiny office he was about to leave, relieved. Joseph nearly yelled in shock and disgust when Haley abruptly emerged from behind a high rack. He abruptly came to a stop, and the blood drained from his cheeks. He started to perspire right away and stumbled back in a rather unmanly swoon. When he spoke, he said, "No, it's not possible. Leave me alone."

To support him, Haley extended a hand. "Can we please have a little conversation, Joseph? I have spent a lot of time looking for you."

"Not right now, not right here. This is where I work. You cannot treat me that way since I didn't enter your father's place of business to try to talk to you at any point. Do you still have the same phone number?"

She backed up her hand and nodded. "Then after I'm done here, I'll give you a call. About ten o'clock will come tonight. Is it too late now?"

She gave a headshake. "That is a plan, all right. Now, unless you want to buy something, I would advise you to leave. If not, I'll contact mall security." He immediately made a U-turn and entered through the "Employees Only" door.

Joseph took a seat at his desk and studied his trembling hands. He wasn't sure if it was out of rage at seeing Haley, rage at her daring to find him, both of the above, or fear that he wouldn't be strong enough to fight her. He didn't know why she was here, but perhaps he needed to find out in order to move forward and put his nightmares to rest.

When he told her he wouldn't be finished before ten, he wasn't kidding. He had discovered comfort in cleaning after everyone had departed ever since the first posting. He would go about the store fixing things, folding clothes and adjusting hanging goods

CHAPTER 16

Before picking up trash and throwing it outside in the dumpster. The store as a whole looked nicer because of the good, honest effort.

He contacted Haley at 9:45 when he was finished. It was a brief exchange of ideas. She was instructed to meet him at a tavern six blocks away from the shop. It was a peaceful area, one of many he had discovered in the many places to which he had been assigned. His main method of finding company outside of work was to find a quiet area to play a game of pool or throw a few darts. He could still only drink a few of beers before getting too drunk and risking a hangover the next morning.

He arrived ahead of Haley and settled into a rear booth. When she arrived, she would be able to see him, but they would also have some privacy.

He could get a good look at her as she searched for him as she came in. Despite the passage of two years, she didn't seem to have changed much. Her weight appeared to be the same, but her haircut had changed slightly. Even if she wasn't wearing much makeup, he wouldn't have noticed anyhow because to her newfound ability to wear little makeup.

She bowed as she approached the table and appeared to kiss him, but he lifted his hands to stop her. She nodded her head as she walked over to the opposite side of the table to take a seat.

"Haley, it's calm now and I'm glad you came. What are you looking for and why are you here?"

She fixed her gaze on his eyes. "That should be self-explanatory, right? I'm trying to find you."

"Okay, we've taken care of that. You located me, I have no idea how or why."

"I guess my main motive was to inquire about your wellbeing. I also wanted to express my regret for what I did on my birthday. Since I was a senior in high school, my family had told me that some people might only desire me for the money I would inherit. Most of the time, I ignored them, but occasionally, someone would approach me as if they were only interested in my money. Despite everything Rose was telling me, I thought you were unique. I initially believed it to be sour apples. She used to complain about him, you, and every other male whenever Jamie would chill up their connection, you know. Then my birthday came, the day I received the majority of my grandmother's trust money, and all of a sudden you proposed to me. You asked me to marry you on the day I got wealthy, even though we had never really ever discussed marriage, having kids, or anything serious."

He waved for her to continue but made no response or comment.

"I truly wasn't going to say anything at that time. I spoke what I was thinking because I was so shocked and, I guess, dismayed that you would genuinely be pursuing my money. Although I don't really recall saying anything, you and the rest of the audience certainly heard me."

Joseph tried to maintain his composure. He understood he wouldn't last long because he never truly possessed a poker face.

When Haley checked in to see how he was handling everything, he remained silent and let her try to fill the void.

"Of course, my dad was fully aware of my thoughts. Before he jumped me and gave me a stern talking to, you had already left. He may have even thought about abandoning me. My other relatives expressed their disappointment to me. They believed that if I wasn't in love with you, I must be some sort of traditional harlot who was only in it for the sex."

My old buddy Rose pulled me aside and assured me that I was acting appropriately. Jamie was shouted at and given many epithets by her, but I believe she was really speaking about you. After standing there for a short while, Jamie began to attack Rose and me. He assured her that just because they weren't dating didn't imply that they didn't share feelings for one another. He told us numerous tales about how you guys used to stick together no matter what. Money, according to him, doesn't make your heart skip a beat. He also revealed to us that you were setting up funds for a down payment on a home for the two of us."

She began to cry and tried to reach out to Joseph with her hands, but he wasn't yet ready to touch her. His hands were still in his lap. She began to sob in public after observing his disgust and didn't appear to be able to stop.

Joseph commenced speaking. "I can understand why you would choose to listen to your best friend. Rose most likely thought about you first. However, I believed that our relationship transcended previous friendships. I had faith in us and believed we were in

90

love. The two of us had spent time getting to know one another. I never requested money from you. Hell, whenever I needed my car serviced, I never even asked your dad for a favor. You didn't even trust me enough to let me know about the trust fund when it came to the money. Instead of trying to surprise you like I did, if I had known that it was bothering you, I would have proposed to you at a different time or begun talking about something long-term. I didn't even let Jamie know what I had in mind. I wanted no one to know beforehand. The true shocker fell on me."

"The day before I left town, Jamie told me about the trust fund. Your money is of no concern to me. If you had been sincere and taken our relationship seriously, I would have happily agreed to a pre-nuptial agreement to protect your financial interests. You, however, lacked confidence and trust in me."

He got up. "I have no idea how you discovered me. You have described how you felt that evening. I'm grateful. I can hopefully put the nightmares behind me now and move on with the remainder of my life." Joseph made a U-turn but stopped. I'll have the bartender call a cab and take you back to your lodging.

He briefly paused at the bar before walking away. When the bartender informed Haley that a cab was ready, she was still sobbing. She thanked her and nodded before blowing her nose. "For what it's worth, sweetheart, that man visits us approximately once per week and never appears to be accompanied by any women. Even if it doesn't look like it went well tonight, you are the first woman we've seen him with."

CHAPTER 17

Haley nodded before getting into a cab to return to her hotel. She had thought that Joseph would take her back to her very luxurious suite after forgiving her. She once more felt hopeless as she walked inside. What did she have in mind? Was she using her wealth to attempt to impress him? Was she showing it off? He entered the suite, where she could see him stand there and laugh at her before turning around to leave. Rose was the only person who hadn't been told that Joseph wasn't interested in her money, after all.

She lazily walked through the sumptuous rooms. What an offer. She was in love with Joseph and eager to begin a life with him when this whole ordeal began. Rose had a sporadic relationship with a man who wasn't responsible enough to commit. Haley was now just a third wheel who was rarely welcomed into Rose and Jamie's home as they got married and prepared to deliver their first child. Rose only saw Haley when Jamie wasn't around because Jamie was open about how he felt for her. After a trip to the store for the new baby, their Girls' Night Out usually consisted of a calm glass of wine at Haley's. Jamie didn't like it, but Haley was going to be the baby's godmother. Since she wasn't planning to have any children just yet, she intended to be the caring aunt and mentor.

Rose required continuous reassurances that Jamie cared for her. Despite Jamie's repeated declarations of love, she felt even more unlovable as a result of her pregnant weight increase. Additionally, Haley had to constantly complimenting her on how gorgeous she was when pregnant. In order to help Rose lose the baby weight and ensure that she was in excellent enough physical condition to give birth, Haley even hired a personal trainer. She ardently hoped that the personal trainer would also be beneficial following Rose's delivery so that Rose may genuinely begin to have a more positive self image.

But right now, Haley's confidence was suffering. However, she had never experienced the nightmare she was currently going through. In her love dreams, when Joseph spotted her, he was overtaken with passion and would quickly grab her in his arms and make her world whole again. Although he appeared receptive to conversation, he didn't respond as she had anticipated.

No, he had truly pretended that she was a friend with whom he really didn't want to interact. How did he say it? Nothing about love, only a few words about faith and trust. Did he no longer adore her? Was she unwilling to accept the truth that he no longer loved her?

She took a seat and talked to herself in depth. She eventually accepted the fact that she had found relationships to be rather simple. In high school, she had cooperated with Lukas until he fucked her. After that, she had been casually dating until she met Arthur. Things were good as long as he decided on their activities and the timing of their sex sessions. She had casually disregarded the rumors that he went sex-trolling when she was busy or didn't truly want to have sex. Since he could obtain anal sex and other kinky things from others, he had never challenged her to engage in such activities. She was simply the sweet girl he walked around with.

Because she wasn't that serious about him, trust had never been a problem. Although he was in some ways a safe haven and the ideal method for her to move on from Lukas, he wasn't the man she wanted to be with her forever.

No, she did not fall in love with the man she desired; instead, she allowed her own fears and Rose's persistent criticism to prevent her from having faith in and trusting Joseph. She had never had any reason to suspect him. He had been completely candid with her, telling her about his past relationships and his desire to take things slowly and fall in love with someone first as friends. He had demonstrated his work ethic to her by working and attending school full-time. She wasn't truly at Rose's fault. Haley was aware that she had the power to silence Rose whenever she was disparaging men in general and Jamie and Joseph in particular. She may have emphasized Joseph's differences from Jamie. She had every reason to put her trust in Joseph.

She was starting to realize and comprehend what Joseph had mentioned. Love wasn't sufficient. When you stop to think about it, that was actually fairly simple. Everybody loves things. Pets, homes, apartments, cars, clothes, shoes, handbags, and other possessions are all things we adore. And up until the next thing appears, we all adore them. But the actual test of a loving relationship was having faith in someone and trusting them with your life, your joy, your sufferings, your disappointments, and even your hopes. Haley had failed, too. She had no faith or trust in Joseph. She had come up far short on the one and only occasion when there might have been a question about his motivations. She had embarrassed him in front of everyone by rejecting his proposal.

She had allowed her own concerns and Rose's prejudiced remarks to determine her future rather than having any faith in her own judgment, her father's judgment, or any faith in Joseph.

She used the opulent ensuite tub to draw herself a hot bath and then relaxed in the bubbles. The bubble piles expanded as she activated the jets, almost overwhelming her. It alleviated her urge to conceal herself from herself and her poor choices. She may refuse to look in the mirror because of the mountains of suds.

Instead, she sought to come up with a plan to meet Joseph again. Perhaps this time they might begin to develop the trust that they so sorely require, as she has come to realize. Thoughts of skepticism crept in. What if he started dating someone new? After all, Joseph rarely appeared in the tavern, according to the bartender. Did he live in a shared apartment?

She struggled out of the tub as the water grew cold, gently dried herself, and then put on a plain t-shirt and some pajamas. The t-shirt belonged to Joseph and was an old one that he had left in her apartment. Unexpectedly, it included one of the graphics he had created. She determined that any of his clothes were fair game because he had not sought to take anything of his from her flat. At originally, they served as a connection point and carried his fragrance. As the months dragged on without any news of him or from him, she eventually started wearing his possessions as a form of self-punishment. Jamie never mentioned their relationship, but she had a suspicion that they still had some sort of connection. Of course, Jamie avoided speaking to Haley directly whenever he could.

She awoke feeling somewhat rested the following morning. Several times in her dreams, a nameless woman would wrap her arms around Joseph and mock her feeble attempts to rekindle their relationship. There was only laughter and arms around Joseph; there was no conversation.

She eventually forced herself out of bed and into the shower. She had time to prepare because she was aware that the store wouldn't open until ten. She sat down and wrote Joseph a note that she would give him if he refused to visit her. She was requesting another meeting at a time that suited him.

She was the first customer to enter the business and searched the area for Joseph, but she was unable to locate him. When she asked a salesperson about Joseph, she learned that he took the day off to pack and prepare his stuff for travel. While Haley was silent, the girl informed her that Joseph will be leaving for a new posting by the end of the week. Haley exhaled with relief. He wasn't fleeing once more; rather, he was moving.

After leaving the note, she proceeded to explore the new city. I was hoping he would call soon.

CHAPTER 18

He did make a call in the late afternoon. When he called, Haley was almost ready to give up on him and face him once again at the store. Joseph agreed to meet for supper this time even though he wasn't really sure what else they needed to discuss. They agreed to meet in the hotel lobby and have dinner in the on-site restaurant, and he emailed her his phone number so she could get in touch with him if necessary. It was said to be a nice location to eat and converse.

When Joseph arrived on schedule, he discovered that Haley had made dinner reservations. They entered and quickly found a seat. Her wine and his whiskey and coke were ordered as their pre-dinner beverages. They didn't talk much after the waiter had subtly left them until they had ordered their entrée.

It was Joseph who got things going. "I admit that I'm a little curious. I received the impression that our discussion was complete and that we could proceed. Although I never heard an apology, I can see your point of view. You didn't want to marry me because you don't love me. I got it. I was merely someone to talk to while waiting for the next man or Arthur to show up. I only wish we had been open and honest with one another about our expectations for this relationship. I may accept the corporate job offer and relocate back to the city now that I have closure, and I assume you have closure as well."

Haley was unaware of this. The idea of Joseph returning to their small city made her smile involuntarily. They would occasionally have to cross paths. Joseph, however, believed the smile to be for a completely other cause. He became quieter as his face darkened. Haley became more depressed as she noticed his altered countenance. It appeared as though a chilling wind had just swept across the space. She extended her hand to his while shuddering. But she didn't touch him.

"Please don't get me wrong; no. I'm grinning at the idea that if you move back, we could occasionally be able to see one another. In actuality, Jamie will be overjoyed. When the time comes, he and Rose want you to serve as the child's godfather." She kept her role as the godmother a secret from him.

Though Joseph assumed Rose was hesitant, he was happy that Jamie had asked him to be his godfather. It was clear from her reply that they would see each other "now and then" that Haley was prepared for a platonic relationship. He nodded. "I suppose I should talk to Jamie and catch up. We hardly ever truly chat, and I barely occasionally text him."

"So you converse with him more than I do, then. Jamie will hardly let me be in the same room with him after the way I treated you. Rose visits my apartment, we do baby shopping together, eat dinner and a drink of wine while we chat about various topics. Rose then returns home to Jamie. About once per week, we get together. Otherwise, when Rose is not around, Jamie starts to become restless. He sometimes acts as like I'm getting her drunk and laid when we go out, I swear."

Joseph gave her a careful look. "Oh no, Rose would never treat Jamie that way. She wouldn't do it even if I tried to take her to a pickup bar. She adores the surface he treads. She actually worries that the extra weight she gained after her pregnancy has made her appear unattractive to him. Both of us are trying to convince her that he still has feelings for her. In order to assist her get in better shape for the latter stages of the pregnancy, childbirth, and possibly afterwards, I have also hired a personal trainer for her. I adore her, but she has such a negative view of herself. Even though Jamie won't talk to me, I want her to be healthy for him and the baby even though I know it's driving him crazy."

Joseph had faith in her. Haley would not participate in a bar pickup scene only for some sex unless something major has changed. And while Rose's attitude would deter most men rather than her weight, he couldn't image her finding someone to take her home.

"I exclusively text Jamie, I guess. Except for my parents, I don't talk to many people on the phone."

After biting her lip for a moment, Haley spoke about her other phobia. "Has your life found a new love?"

"No, although I have dated a few people, none of them ever seemed to have the spark I was searching for. I've only ever dated someone for ten dates at most. Naturally, the fact that I rarely stay in one place for longer than six to eight months has an impact on any new relationships."

Why haven't you made a home anywhere since you left?

CHAPTER 19

"I can now solve issues. I'm deployed to failed or struggling businesses to look for ways to increase profits. I'll move on to the next store once it appears better on the books. A few of the many stores in our chain are having issues. Although we don't want to, it's just a matter of business. If your performance falls short of expectations, action must be taken. It is anticipated that each store bears its own weight."

"I understand their desire for you to return to corporate. Have you been prosperous in every store?"

"So far. I started with the one that wasn't doing as well and quickly improved it. There was a lot of dead weight that needed to be removed, and corporate needed to deal with diversity training. It felt like a new store with a fresh outlook and more marketing. The management promised to continue the excellent work."

"I would expect that you would have your pick of attractive and sexy women given the attractive sales crew and target consumer demographic you are aiming for."

Joseph let out a shoulder shrug. "I guess. Simply said, there hasn't been much time or interest. I put in between 12 and 14 hours every day. I usually arrive about eight and leave after 10. By the end of the day, I'm generally worn out and lack the willpower to go out and find company."

"It's a shame. You shouldn't have to exert yourself so much. Can't they offer some assistance?"

"Corporate does its best efforts, yet it seems that one person can have a bigger impact than an entire staff. That idea was tested. In reality, because their ideas had failed, the majority of the administration had anticipated me to fail when I offered to visit the chain's worst-performing store."

During the course of their meal, he changed the topic. "Inform me of your condition. How is your dad doing?"

Haley responded and then began to eat. It took some time because she had always been instructed not to speak while she had her mouth full. "Dad is good. He is actually more than fine. He met a woman who was struggling financially and need major engine repairs. He fell in love with her and asked her out as he was figuring up a payback strategy. Since then, they have only been together, and they don't seem prepared to change their status at the moment. Dad frequently inquires about you. The majority of the chats then turn into an indictment of how I injured you."

Joseph simply shrugged and continued to devour his steak. Haley took note of that but didn't say anything to Joseph other than to carry on. "For my part, I'm doing a better job of marketing the company. We have achieved success. Since so many of our customers are women, I initially suggested a beefcake calendar. No nudity, although some of the most attractive mechanics had their shirts off and were greased to make sweaty marks for the photographs. We did it again the next year since it was so well-liked. We are currently expanding our repair network and have joined a large national tire chain. We still have access to any brand a customer want while passing along savings on our name-brand tires."

Joseph paused. "Is there somebody special in your life? Has Arthur ever returned?"

Haley raised an eyebrow in shock. Why do you think I'm pining for Arthur, I ask?

Marc shrugged. "I'm not sure. Prior to me, you dated and knew him. It appeared like you were only over him because he made the decision to go after his dreams, not necessarily because you were. Initially, I thought of myself as merely someone to spend around with till his return."

Haley put down her fork. She suddenly lost her appetite. "NO, No! That's untrue. You were never meant to take the place of Arthur. I was relieved that he made the decision to go since I knew that we had no future together. I was afraid he might make me a proposal. Yes, I really loved him, but he wasn't going to be my future love interest. If anything, I utilized him to help me mature a bit. You are the only one I love. I never date. Since I insulted you and drove you away, I haven't been made to do anything sexual. Since then, I've been critical of myself for my lack of faith and confidence. Last night, when you began to discuss that very topic, I was horrified with myself."

Her face began to abruptly become wet. " That's pretty much it. Rose wasn't at fault. She was depressed, lonely, and believed that no man cared about her. No, I didn't stand up for you and order her to stop abusing you. I allowed it to continue and began to distrust myself in addition to my own failings. I didn't believe in how I felt about you. I had no faith in you. I never got the impression from you that you were only pursuing my money. I had no confidence in us or you. We were destroyed by my doubts, and I would spend every penny I have to repair us."

She quickly stood up and walked out of the eatery. Joseph was perplexed. He had imagined that she was in love with Arthur and was just waiting for him to come back at this point. He was only dreaming when he saw them laughing in his dreams. Who, then, lacked faith and trust? He may not have had any faith in her or any hope that there might have been a misunderstanding if he hadn't moved away right away after the mess involving his marriage proposal. In his sorrow and shame, Jamie had tried to explain to him a straightforward explanation for the mistake, but he wouldn't listen.

He placed a second drink order and returned the leftover meal with praises and apologies. Despite having no hunger, he felt he wanted another drink. While sipping the mixture gently, he thought about what Haley had said. He felt a little self-conscious. He could hold her responsible for her lack of trust and faith, but he was also clearly at fault. He hadn't treated any of his staff members the same way he did Haley. Even though he was aware that someone had to be let go, he had each person come into his office to address the reasons for dismissal. Even those who had faced prosecution had been given opportunity to talk to him about their mistakes. He could now understand how his lack of respect for Haley had led him to simply get up and leave without giving her a chance to defend herself. Actually, perhaps she had wanted to talk about what had happened since she had made attempts to contact him in the days following the birthday celebration. She was no longer a part of his life at all.

He finished his drink and departed the establishment. Haley's room number was obviously not given to him by the counter workers, so he left a message asking her to call him.

Haley exited the elevator and started to look around as he turned to go. Joseph had a sneaking suspicion that she wasn't necessarily looking for him, but rather a lover. That uncertainty was dispelled, though, by the expression on her face when she saw him standing by the front entrance. She smiled brightly, but it also had a nervous quality to it, as if she was worried he may go away. He noticed that he was beginning to smile back. They gathered in the center of the spacious lobby and settled into several plush chairs there.

Now that they had met, the talk was much less passionate and more of an informal, cordial desire to get to know each other. They felt much more at ease with one another. No attempts were made to touch or make any kind of cutesy comments to one another. That might be postponed until later.

Joseph was able to reveal to Haley his own failings as they conversed. He expressed regret for not allowing her to speak with him after the celebration. She had accidentally made him feel humiliated, and he recognized his own lack of maturity. She got up from her chair, knelt down in front of him, and asked for his pardon. They may have appeared to be arguing about who should forgive whom if someone had been nearby and listening.

At last, Joseph seized Haley, sat her on his lap, and kissed her into submission. When he turned around, two employees at the desk were grinning at them while the other two were wishing they were out of sight of the public. Joseph recommended that they go for a walk. The streets were well lit and the hotel was located in an area with a large police presence so late evening walks were not discouraged.

They window shopped as they talked and walked. It was becoming more friendly and lively as they continued down the street.

Haley finally broached the subject she wanted an answer to. "Have you decided about taking the corporate office job?"

Joseph let out a shoulder shrug. "I'm not sure. This time of helping stores has presented me with a great opportunity to grow and learn. The short time at each store doesn't make my personal life easier and I don't have time to make new friends. But I believe I am actually making a difference, especially on the very poor performing stores and I take solace in that."

Haley could see that this was the Joseph that she first knew and probably had fallen in love with. His focus on the problem and then seeing to its successful conclusion was what helped make him successful.

"Can you not do the same thing at the home office?"

He shrugged his shoulders again. "I'm not sure. I was the assistant manager of the local store when we broke up. I had worked in

CHAPTER 20

various departments at the headquarters just to learn as much as possible but I didn't see my self there. Since I have made myself into a problem solver I don't know if there is that much work at headquarters that needs my kind of skill. It might be time to go free-lance, kind of like a systems analyst. I could market myself as the go-to problem solver for any company."

Haley stopped walking and turned to face him. "Maybe that is your future. Why don't we try it out?"

Joseph had to stop because she was in front of him. "What do you mean?"

She was silent for a few moments. "Take my dad's business for example. We are doing okay but not as well as I would like. I, and Dad, for that matter, don't expect to be Pep Boys but we want to be successful with every shop. Some of the new shops are testimonials to the industry, nice and new and shiny with the newest equipment but they are not as profitable as we would like them to be. The older shops are more profitable but don't look the newest and brightest."

Joseph started to walk again but was quiet as he did so. Haley grabbed his arm and put it around her waist, like she had always wanted to. When he moved slightly away she shook her head and snuggled closer. They just couldn't walk very fast doing this but she was feeling loved and treasured with his arm around her.

Joseph asked a few questions. "The new stores, who made the decision about what they would look like?"

"The architect did."

"Does he or she know anything about auto mechanics and repair shops?"

"I suppose not. Dad has been more than one comment about how work doesn't flow well in the new buildings."

"When were the older buildings last updated and remodeled?"

"Actually I don't believe any have been remodeled since opening."

"I would have to study the business and how things are done for a while but I would think that the older buildings need remodeled for a new and attractive look to bring in new customers. All of the shops need the best and newest equipment to compete with any other in the chain along with any other repair shop in the region. The new buildings might just need a retooling to make work flow easier and reduce wasted time." He stopped talking for a moment. "Where do you get your parts from?"

"A national chain mostly. We order and anything they don't keep on hand comes in the next day."

"Have you thought about becoming a franchise of the national chain and then have parts immediately available along with the repairs?"

"I believe dad thought about that once upon a time but not lately, why?"

"With the number of shops that need constant parts and supplies the cost per part might go down and you wouldn't have to rely on another company's delivery people to get parts to the shops as needed. If you had a store attached to the shop that had common parts right there then turn-around on repairs might go down. It would have to be studied at length as it would be a large capital outlay."

Haley stopped him again and gave him a kiss. "See, you haven't even stepped foot in the shops in two years but have great ideas on how to improve repair times and maybe even the bottom line. Would you like a contract for your consultant work?"

Joseph gave in and kissed her back. "I don't know yet but your offer is tempting. I suppose if I come back to the corporate offices I could work on your project in the evenings and weekends."

They smiled at each other and headed back to the hotel as it was getting quite late.

No, they didn't immediately get back to an intimate level. It took time and a lot of effort on their part to rebuild their relationship.

Joseph did spend a couple of months on the next store before accepting the corporate job. When he returned to the city he had Haley find a house to purchase. With the raises, bonuses and savings he was able to purchase the house with cash and make the upgrades that Haley wanted to make it a more comfortable home. They had not talked about any kind of permanent arrangement since starting to talk with each other again. They were taking it slow. Haley's family welcomed Joseph back as though he had never left. Haley actually remarked that her family seemed to like Joseph more than her then she smiled and giggled. She was maturing and not as shallow as she had been.

Haley's dad had then approached Joseph about the subject of his shops. Joseph worked long hours on weekends and evenings to understand the needs of the technicians before making recommendations. Brian had cringed at the cost of remodeling and upgrading but realized that it was necessary to compete. His oldest shop was the first to get completely renovated. This was his corporate headquarters as well and the new look was greatly appreciated by both customers and his employees.

The idea of becoming a franchise of a national parts chain was put aside as too complicated for the moment until the idea of creating a holding company was put forward. The holding company could become the owners of the parts stores and put one next to each shop for quick delivery of parts but also be available for the shade tree mechanic and other shops. Parts would be wholesaled to the repair shops, all of them, competitors and Brian's alike.

It had been almost a year since Haley and Joseph had made peace with each other. They now were communicating better. They were telling each other their dreams and aspirations, something that had been missing before. They were also intimate again. Their sex life was better than before with their new communication level.

Finally Joseph came over to Haley's apartment one evening. For once Rose, the new baby girl, Stacie, and Jamie weren't visiting. Since Joseph had come home Jamie had forgiven Haley and had fully embraced the idea of her being godmother as long as Joseph had agreed to be godfather. Joseph had wholeheartedly agreed.

After giving her a kiss and a little fondling he had Haley sit down at the table. "I have something important to discuss with you, if I may." She nodded.

Joseph slid a paper over to her. "This is a pre-nuptial agreement. Basically it says that whatever assets we each have coming into a marriage remains that person's property and is exempt from any judgment if we should break up. It also lays out the way increases in assets, such as a house, cars, boats, campers, and other assets should we decide to quit the marriage. There are penalties in case of infidelity. My lawyer says this is pretty much a standard practice these days."

Haley became a little upset and threw the paper back to Joseph. "I don't want it."

Joseph smiled at her. "Too bad. I do. I don't want you, any of your family, you dad, or Rose misunderstanding why I want to marry you. If you look on the back side of the paper you will see that I have already signed it and notarized it. It only needs your signature and notary signature and it will be filed with the court." He slid the paper back to her.

"No, no, no! I don't want that. I trust you and I have faith in you. I know you aren't after my money. Haven't we gotten past this yet? Is this going to be always between us?"

He smiled at her. "No, it won't. Just sign this or better yet take it to your dad's attorney and have him look it over and we can negotiate some points but I want the basic parts of this to stand."

She was getting more upset and leaned back with her arms crossed. "No, I will not sign any prenuptial agreement, not here, not now, not ever."

"Do you want to marry me?"

"More than anything else in the world."

"Then why would you be against something that would protect you in case we don't work out? I don't want your money. I am earning enough to live on and our combined income will assure that we live comfortably. You can then use you money any way you decide. If you want to pay for vacations, you can. If you want to make sure our children have education money you can set up trust funds. It will be your decision. I would hope that you would discuss spending and investments with me but it would protect you."

Haley was adamant. "No, it will be our money, not my money. I will not keep anything from you. We will be full partners in everything we do. Not only the trust fund but if I inherit the businesses I want you to be my full partner in running them. You and I will share equally in everything."

Joseph set aside the paper for a moment. "Will you do me the honor of becoming my wife?"

Haley jumped up and ran around the table and plopped herself in Joseph's lap. "Yes, I will and I do." She gave him a long kiss that was as full of passion as she could muster.

When they finally came up for air Joseph let her know his plans for the next day. "Tomorrow we should go ring shopping to find the perfect ring for you."

Haley gave him a shy smile. She kissed him again and got up from his lap and went into her bedroom. When she came out she was carrying a ring box. She gave it to Joseph. "What is this? Some kind of ring for me to wear?"

"No, silly, it is my ring. I want you to put it on my finger. When you left Jamie brought me the ring and told me how you wanted him to take it and give it to Rose. He and she discussed it and decided they wanted their own ring, not one that would be associated with pain and sorrow. I used to wear it around my neck on a necklace just to remind me what kind of witch I had been to you. When we got back together I put it back in the box hoping you would ask me again to marry you."

He opened the box and then got down on his knee. "Haley will you marry me?" She nodded and he placed the ring on her finger. He stood and kissed her again. "Shall we go out for supper?"

"Nope, we are going to call all of yours and my families and announce that I finally got my head out of my ass. I think we will go over to Dad's first and then burn up the phones."

Joseph smiled and agreed. Surreptitiously he put the pre-nup in his pocket. He was sure that Brian would talk some sense into Haley before the wedding.

All was well.

THE END

Lightning Source UK Ltd.
Milton Keynes UK
UKHW010010131222
413832UK00002BA/37